CAL

SECRETS AND LIES SERIES BOOK 1

B J ALPHA

CAL

Secrets and Lies Series Book 1

Copyright @ 2021 by BJ Alpha

Published by BJ Alpha

Edited by Tanya Oemig

Cover Design by Katie Evans

❀ Created with Vellum

"If you've met one individual with autism, you've met one individual with autism."

Stephen Shore

CAL

Secrets and Lies

Book 1

PROLOGUE

Oscar

I glare at the multiple screens as the images shake. I take a deep breath knowing the inevitable is about to happen, again. My servers crash. *Fuck*!

The bastard doing this is going to go down. I already have a plan and it's going to be fucking epic. This last hit is a step too far, motherfucker. Fifty million dollars too far to be precise. This isn't a small amount anymore, no, the fucker tested our limits and now he was going for the big bucks.

I look up at the blank screen and the fucking prick's signature little cartoon cat strolls across my screen with a pacifier in its mouth and proceeds to spit the damn thing out and cry tears in bucketloads. What a piss-taking piece of shit this dick is. Well, this is the last time because he doesn't know what's going to hit him. Within the next twenty-four hours, the little prick is going to learn one hell of a lesson and not just from us.

My phone lights up. I know instantly my brother is going

to be shouting shit at me, wanting answers to his latest bank alert letting him know he is down ten million. At least this time I can tell him I have the cunt.

Thanks to my new friend, redcars, kittykat is about to be taken down. And I can't wait to see it up close and personal.

CHAPTER 1

Lily

Wow. I walk out of the salon feeling like a new woman. Okay, a little dramatic but seriously, when was the last time I was pampered like this? I have a spring in my step and an internal glow. Is that even possible? Sure feels like it.

I can't help but smile as I make my way across the parking lot. It's pitch black and a pretty shitty night, but my son Reece has made me feel I'm on cloud nine. I can honestly say that has never happened—like literally never!

I'm sure he is still sucking up from his last school fuck-up, but I can't hold it against him forever. I just wish he realized how bad the things he did are. I wish he wouldn't keep screwing up and for him to hold some accountability for his actions. But let's face it, that is never going to happen.

I decide to look at the positive side of things. The boy had done good. How many other teenager's mothers received a card saying they were booked into a spa-salon for the evening, paid for by doing odd jobs for neighbors on the complex we lived at? Not many, I'm sure.

I glance at my phone and realize I'm going to be home earlier than expected. That was okay—Reece had texted he was ordering pizza for our supper. Another treat, apparently.

Perhaps things were starting to change? Perhaps things were finally starting to look fucking up? I couldn't be too optimistic because, let's face it, I'd had a haircut!

I unlock the car and throw my bag on the passenger seat, smiling as I start the engine. As I'm about to pull out, my phone buzzes in the cup holder. I glance at it and in those split seconds my whole world shatters into a thousand pieces.

Reece: BLACKBIRD

One word in a text from my son and I know yet again my life will never be the same.

I drive home as fast as I can. Anxiety ripples through me as I go through what I have to do when I arrive. I hope and pray Reece has remembered everything we'd agreed. Who am I kidding? Reece set these procedures in place and I follow them.

I pull up farther away than normal, toward the fire escape, and look up to our third-floor corner apartment. The light is on and it is quiet as normal. I scan the area. No one hanging around and only the odd car in the parking lot. I open my bag and take the handgun out, grab my phone, and make my way to the fire exit.

I take a deep breath and do our signature whistle twice, waiting to see if the next stage of our plan will emerge. I only hope I'm not too late.

Less than a minute later, the power goes off, giving me exactly two minutes to enter the building and apartment undetected. I race up the stairs and open the fire exit with the key Reece had proudly presented to me only a couple of weeks ago. Did I question it at the time? No, why the hell would I? The kid was always doing cunning and odd things. I struggled to keep up with him the best of times, but when he was plotting? Puff, the kid blew my mind and I didn't have the time nor energy to try and analyze his motives.

I'm inside the building and making my way toward the door. Pausing, I can hear raised voices and my son's...laugh? He didn't sound in danger but the other two voices are authoritative and pissed. I knew instantly that Reece didn't understand that he was in danger. I gently open the door and see a tall shadow near the table at the end of our small apartment. He's turned toward the corner of the room where I can hear Reece's voice mumbling.

If they've hurt my baby I swear to god I will have no problem blowing the motherfucker's brains out on my dining table.

I creep toward the shadow, staying low behind the kitchen counter and using it as a shield. I get right up to the guy and crack the gun's safety off, holding the gun directly under the back of his neck just as the generator kicks in and the lights flick back on.

"Mom, about fucking time!"

I quickly scan the scene in front of me. Reece is slumped with his arms tied at the wrist to a chair and his ankles tied to the chair legs. He has a small cut on his lip but doesn't appear to be hurt anywhere else, just anxious.

A guy is standing next to him—tall, lean, with thick dark hair, long on top, and glasses. He looks handsomely intelligent. His body language gives an odd pissed-off vibe with his arms crossed in front of him, ready for a confrontation.

The guy I have the gun up to is fucking huge, like Hulk

huge. I can barely reach his neck, but I wasn't about to move, not when these fuckers had my baby strapped up like a sacrificial lamb.

"Who the fuck are you? Untie my son you bastards!" I spit.

Reece sighs. "Mom, it's okay. Calm down."

Was he serious? Calm down? Calm down? I can barely freaking think.

"What's happening? What do you want with my son? Untie him now otherwise I'll pull the fucking trigger!"

The guy next to Reece takes a step forward, making me jump. "Your son is in serious trouble and we want some answers, now," he firmly asserts with a coolness I only wish I could imitate.

"Jesus, Reece, what the hell have you done?"

Reece takes a deep breath. Just as he is about to open his mouth, the door bursts open, making me shriek. A guy walks toward me with a gun aimed at my head and then stops midway when he sees I also have a gun pointed toward Hulk's head.

He slows his pace, lowers his weapon, and begins to move his head from side to side as if trying to scrutinize me. What the hell is happening?

CHAPTER 2

Cal

I burst through the door. I'd been waiting in the car but saw the shadowed figure enter the fire escape once the lights went out. Yeah, not on my watch, fuckwit.

Oscar had said it would be a quick in and out job so I figured I'd wait this one out.

I realize instantly a woman points a gun to the back of Brennan's head. What fucking bitch dare put a gun to the back of my brother? I take her in as she glances from me to Oscar and a kid in a chair. The kid is clearly a teenager— fifteen, maybe sixteen. He's slouched with basketball shorts and a baggy T-shirt on, a cap back to front, and strapped to the chair in typical Oscar torture fashion.

I look again at the woman, something about her so familiar. When she looks me directly in the eye, my heart races. I know without a shadow of a doubt it's her.

"Carmen? Is that you?" She glares at me and those beautiful green eyes of hers pop out of her head with recognition. Wow. She is just...wow! Her long dark hair flows down her back in waves. She is still petite, wearing some ripped jeans and Converse with a white vest top and leather jacket. She is fucking perfect, still.

"Cal? What the hell are you doing here? What the hell is happening?" She's clearly panicking.

"Oscar, what's happening?" I ask my brother, who's standing beside the kid. Her brother maybe?

Oscar rubs his jaw and replies rather sheepishly, "The boy. It's him. He's kittykat," he replies, pointing toward the kid.

I calm my voice. "Carmen, I need you to put the gun down."

"Untie my son," she counters, her sharp intake of breath giving away her nerves.

"Her name's not fucking Carmen, you dumb dick," the kid scoffs, making me spin to fully face him.

"Reece, what the hell is happening here?" she asks, a shake in her voice.

"Mom, go over to the counter. I put a cup there with water. Take the Valium with it," he says nonchalantly, like he's talking about popping candy in his mouth.

"Reece, what the hell are you talking about? What the hell have you done? It's bad, isn't it? I know it is, just fucking tell me!" she shrieks.

Wait, did he just call her Mom? Carmen has a kid? A fucking big dumbass kid by looking at him. I didn't know that. She never mentioned him, not once.

"I thought I was doing you a favor okay? You know, so you could finish your degree? I got you some money and these guys are a little pissed about it, that's all. It was yours anyway, they owed it to you. Well, one of them did at least. I mean, I wasn't sure which one at the time, but I guess I am now," he said grumbling and rambling to himself.

Owed it to them? What the hell is he on with? He took our money? This jumped-up punk took our money?

"I'm sorry, honey, but what the hell are you talking about?" Carmen's eyebrows furrow with uncertainty. She's calmer than before, clearly trying a different tactic with the kid.

"You got me to take biology, not me. I didn't even want to do the damn subject. It's boring as shit. Not my fault I found what I found. Anyway, you should be happy you have your degree money so..." He shrugs.

This kid speaks in fucking riddles, fast jumbled up fucking riddles, and I am exasperated just listening to him, trying to take it in.

"Reece, honey, you really need to explain things a little easier. I don't understand what you're telling me. Are you saying you took these guys' money?" She waves the gun in our direction, making me nervous as fuck.

I mean come on, Carmen. I thought we'd established that. The little shit has been filtering our money for months now but after the big hit we took yesterday...Yeah, no fucker gets away with that.

He takes a deep breath and rolls his eyes as if he's about to explain to a child. "Look, I was doing my biology home-work and figured I'd do a DNA trace. You know, to get you your child support to finish your degree. One thing led to another and I narrowed it down to these dicks' family. I mean, I couldn't say which one owed you for sure because there's like five of them. I did check their blood types to try and match us but that didn't straighten things out either, so I figured I'd hit them all up and make them pay," he says with a shrug as if it was fucking nothing.

I rub my hand through my hair in confusion. What the hell, what? One of us is his fucking dad?

Oh. Sweet. Fucking. Jesus. No.

"Carmen, what the hell is he talking about? How old is he? What is he trying to say?" I say, shaking with panic blossoming inside.

She turns to me painfully slow with her head hanging down. She slowly looks up at me, those fucking beautiful eyes full of sympathy.

"I...I...I don't know what to say. I didn't know about any of this. I swear to you, Cal, I didn't know he was doing any of this. I didn't even know your full fucking name for god's sake!"

"He's my fucking son?" I choke out, looking at the smug little shit. How the fuck have I created him?

She nods with her head down, looking defeated as she lowers the gun. Bren turns to face me with his eyebrows in his hairline, letting out a breath of air he'd been holding in and becoming anxious as hell.

"Blood groups were Bren A positive, Cal A positive, Oscar B positive, Finn A positive, and Connor B positive," the kid says nonchalantly as if explaining further. "Anyway, the sixty million I took wasn't much to you guys so I don't know why the fuck you're so pissed. I've a feeling it's more a pride thing, am I right?" he says, sniggering.

Oscar's head snaps up, "$60 million?"

The little lunatic starts laughing. "Oh shit! Wow, I thought you were meant to be the clever little hacker," he mocks. "Jesus! Yeah, I figured I'd swipe a ten from your daddy too. You know the offshore account ending 3452? Yeah, didn't think I'd be able to access those, did ya? Dumb fuck." The little prick is shaking his head, laughing to himself. Oscar's face pales and he takes a step back, almost staggering. Me? I'm fucking empty, empty. Like what the fuck is happening here?

The next little clusterfuck occurs instantly. The kid's hand pops up off the chair arm. Throwing the ropes off and untying his other arm, he then proceeds to bend down to his socks, whips a penknife out, and cuts the ties on his ankles. We all watched open-mouthed, Oscar's face falls and he looks from me to the kid in question.

The kid huffs and glares at Oscar. "Next time use a Palomar knot, you dumb dick." He shakes his head, apparently disgusted by Oscar's lack of knot skills. It's never been a problem before but what the fuck do we know?

We watch him as he marches to the kitchen counter, taking his hat off in the process and throwing it on the couch. We look at him and then at each other. We're all thinking the same thing...the kid's thick, short, wavy, black hair that he's now tugging is my fucking hair! He's my fucking double.

His size, shitty attitude, smug fucking smirk, bright blue eyes, and the fucking hair. He grabs the glass of water and pill, grumbling to himself. Clearly annoyed, he places it in front of Carmen, who is now sitting at the table with her head in her hands.

He goes to the couch next to the chair he'd been strapped in and throws himself down.

"Mom, I think you should take the drink and pill and let's get this shit over with. You're already a little on edge."

"On edge, on fucking edge, are you kidding me right now, Reece?" She glares at him with venom in her eyes as he ducks his head down, pulling at his hair. Clearly, this is a nervous thing. It's something I do a lot too.

Silence descends the room as we all stare at the mini-me.

"Oh, my fucking god, no!" she screeches, making us all jump in the process. "There's fucking more, isn't there? I can't cope, I swear to fucking god I can't cope, Reece!" She's getting hysterical.

Calmly I figure I'd better say something to try and ease the situation. It can't get much worse than this, right? "Carmen, take some deep breaths and try and calm down a little, hey?"

Well, that was apparently the wrong thing to say because....*boom!* The fucking kid virtually spits and screams at me, "Her name is fucking Lily, not Carmen, you dumb fuck. Jesus, why the hell did I get the thick one? Why couldn't it have been him?" He gestures toward Oscar, who is just as shocked as me at this outburst.

Oscar's face screams relief. Relief that he hasn't spawned the god damn little Satan. Bren chuckles. "You are so in the shit, man." I shake my head at him. Trust him to revel in my fucking downfall.

I take a deep breath and try and analyze what I've discovered. So, her name is Lily?

Honestly, it suits her. I told her I didn't feel comfortable with her being called Carmen, but I got it. I had to earn her trust. And I never got the chance to follow that through.

LILY

I know my son and I know there is more to come. He didn't just offer me Valium for no reason. The last time I had those I was in a pretty bad way, back when our lives had been shattered and I never thought we'd get through it.

No, he wouldn't offer me those without a plausible explanation. Thing is, I don't want to know.

Cal appears dumbstruck. He's in his own little world, absolutely fucking dumbstruck.

I look over to both the guys, Cal's brothers I guess. Hulk looks slightly amused by the whole situation and keeps looking at Reece and then Cal, shaking his head and laughing to himself, clearly gobsmacked at Cal's mini-me. The leaner one—Oscar? He keeps looking at Reece...in awe? Intrigued, maybe? He's watching and analyzing his every move.

I clear my throat. *Time to man up, Lily, rip off the Band-Aid and deal with this shit.*

"Reece, what's going on, honey?" I say it in a calm and sweet way because I know my son and if Reece sees or hears distress in me, he shuts down and panics. It could throw him into one of his meltdowns and I seriously could not cope with that shit at this moment.

"It's not my fault, Mom. It's his, he set me up!" He throws up his arms toward Oscar, who jumps at the accusation.

Oscar's face morphs into terror. "Oh shit!" he responds as he steps back, stunned at Reece's words.

"What does he mean, you set him up? What's going on, Reece?"

All the men look at one another and they seem to realize something I don't know anything about.

"They set the cartel onto us, Mom!" Reece replies, desperation in his voice.

CHAPTER 3

Cal

H *oly. Fucking. Shit.* What the hell have we done?

Lily jumps up and wails before almost collapsing at the side of the table. I catch her just in time before she slumps into my arms. She buries her head in her hands, gently rocking back and forth, doing a breathing exercise to calm herself in the process.

A few minutes pass where we say nothing, all too shocked at the events.

We look at one another and then at Reece, who seems to be dealing with things better than you'd expect. He seems quite...unfazed. There is something fucking wrong with this kid. I need to find out more that's for sure.

"It's okay, Mom. That's why I brought them here to help us. They can help us!"

At that statement, Oscar's spine straightens and he chimes in, "Reece, what do you mean, you brought us here?"

"You know what I mean—fed you the intel, like breadcrumbs, to find us." He rolls his eyes at my brother's apparently stupid question.

So, the kid is saying he led us here? I thought Oscar had a lead via a fellow hacker.

Whatever, I sure as hell don't understand that shit. I shake my head, struggling to understand what the hell is happening.

Lily rises to her feet, seemingly finding new confidence to deal with the next onslaught her son—our son—has brought to her door.

"I...I can't deal with the cartel again, Reece. That shit nearly killed me the last time. What the fuck are we going to do?" She begins to cry again and paces up and down the room, her beautiful face marred with tears.

Oscar clears his throat and strokes his chin in thought. "Reece buddy, have you had any contact within the last forty-eight hours from anyone outside your usual circle? Any evidence something is amiss? Anything that may lead directly to the cartel being at your door anytime soon?"

"No. I've got eyes via all surveillance within a twenty-mile radius to give us a head start. The private jet they keep at the nearest airport left yesterday, which is why I wanted to bump things along with hitting you guys up harder. It hasn't returned as of yet but I'm estimating within the next twenty-four hours, things are going to change." He speaks fluently, with confidence, as though he's reporting a job back to management. He's clear, concise, and certain. Oscar nods, impressed with Reece's response.

Reece's voice softens. "Mom, I packed your bag. It's on your bed. My medication is in there too. If you need the toilet you need to go soon. We have to leave and it's going to be a long journey." He talks to her as though she's the child.

Lily nods her head, dazed. She leaves the room and goes to the bathroom like a zombie.

Reece shoots up off the couch like an excitable child going on a field trip. "Pussy, Pussy, Pussy," he chants.

My head spins toward Bren, who is wide-fucking-eyed, then at Oscar, who shrugs. What the living fuck was he on with now? He walks up and down the apartment opening the doors that I assume are bedrooms and sharply shouts, "Pussy!"

I sit on a chair, rubbing my head. I have the mother of all goddamn headaches and I'm as confused as hell. The lunatic popping in and out the doors is getting louder. "Pussy!"

"What the fuck is he going on about?" I ask nobody in particular.

Lily pops her head out the door. "He's looking for his cat."

"You let him call the cat Pussy?" Bren asks, both shocked and amused, snorting at his question.

"Yes, I did, because you know what, you learn to choose your battles with a child like Reece."

"What year is Reece in school, Lily?" Oscar asks. Good question. I hadn't asked a fucking thing. I'm still coming to terms with the fact the little punk is mine.

She looks down and then up again, something I notice she does when she's uncomfortable. "He isn't in school at the minute."

"You homeschool him?" I ask, surprised.

She spins around and glares at me with utter venom coming out of her eyeballs. "No! I do not fucking home-school him. Seriously, how the fuck am I supposed to home-school him? I can't teach him jackshit! Jesus, they couldn't teach him jackshit," she spits out.

I put my hands up in defense. "Lily, Jesus, I didn't mean anything by it."

"You're right. I'm sorry. I'm a little on edge. He's recently been let go from school due to an incident there and I'm still coming to terms with the drama from that, that's all. I'm sorry," she mumbles.

Bren pipes up. "So, he got kicked out. Is that what you're saying?" Both Lily and I shoot him a look, a shut-the-fuck-up look.

Reece returns to the room with a fat brown tiger cat in his arms, grinning and nuzzling it as a toddler would. Clearly the kid loves his cat. I laugh to myself at the sight of this strapping teenager and his cherished cat.

"Yeah, they kicked me out, the dicks," he replies to Bren. "Wasn't even my fault. I was only sticking up for my mom." My brothers and I look at one another, raise our eyebrows, and roll our eyes because it appears Reece doesn't take any responsibility for his actions. It is always someone else's fault.

LILY

I walk over to Reece and stroke the cat. I whisper into Reece's ear, "Reece honey, can you go and get a burner... *sdelat' eto dva.*" I slip into Russian and hold up two fingers to indicate he bring two. He nods and returns to his bedroom.

"The cat's a therapy cat." I figured I'd better clear that up. Bren snorts and I roll my eyes in response. I'm used to idiots that don't understand and frankly I don't give a shit.

"So, Reece is high-functioning, am I right?" Oscar asks. Honestly, I'm freaking relieved someone might have an idea of what it is I'm dealing with.

"Yeah, he is." I look at Cal to try and get him to understand his son is a little different than other kids his age.

"He barely has any concept of interpersonal skills, cannot read a situation the same way we do, and will struggle to grasp emotion and the repercussions of his actions."

"Clearly," Bren responds sarcastically.

Bren doesn't say much apart from his stupid comments now and then, but that's okay. I can tune that shit out.

Cal looks at me as though I'm an alien. Nope, not an

ounce of that went in, did it? I exhale. This is going to be hard fucking work.

"His IT skills are second to none, Lily. Seriously, I've never seen anything like it...ever. I thought I was good, but the kid has had me on a runaround for months now, and he speaks as though he set this up. I mean, seriously, is he capable of that?"

"Without a shadow of a doubt, Oscar. What you see is only the tip of a huge iceberg. You're going to be a lot more surprised, believe me."

Oscar rubs his hand along his jaw, taking it all in.

"What else?" Cal asks, waving his hands around. I'm a little taken aback because frankly, I thought he'd zoned out.

"He doesn't like touching, he's hypersensitive to foods, has daily rituals, talks endlessly. He has sleep apnea. The list goes on, Cal." I sigh. How do you put it all in a sentence and give an answer? I've grown to accept Reece's traits and triggers and we work together to make life as easy and comfortable as possible for us both.

"We really should be getting going," Oscar surmises. I exhale and look around the apartment. The pizza is on the counter. My mug from this morning is still in the sink. Everything is how we left it and now we were going to go, again. Nothing is ever going to be the same. Time for yet another fresh start. At least this time we aren't doing it alone.

CHAPTER 4

Cal

Lily turns around in the apartment slowly, taking everything in. She looks completely overwhelmed and devastated. Her son has just obliterated her life and turned it upside down and he doesn't appear to give a fuck.

I walk over to her and lift her chin with my finger. Looking into those beautiful green eyes I say, "It's going to be ok, Lily. We've got you."

She looks me in the eye, tears brimming. Jesus, she looks so pained and it hurts to see it. How can she look at me like that and it hurt me so much? I gulp, a deep ache in my chest tightening.

"Come on, let's get you guys in the car." I nod toward the door.

Lily turns and nods to Reece, who has now put his AirPods in and seems quite happy with the turn of events. Bren grabs the bags and the fucking cat in its cage.

Oscar walks behind Reece. My brother doesn't deal with

people very well. That's why he's always dealt with the IT side of things but he appears to relate to Reece. Already I can see my brother has taken him under his wing. He glances at me and nods as if to say *I've got him.*

I smile at him weakly. I don't feel much like smiling but I'm grateful for him being here, for both of my brothers being here.

We get to the SUV and Bren takes the driver's seat.

Oscar is riding upfront and that puts me in the back with Lily. Reece is behind us with the cat.

"Where are we even going?" Lily finally asks. She sounds broken and I don't think she's even registered leaving the apartment and getting in the car.

Oscar speaks up. He is already busy working on his tablet, making arrangements and putting things in place. "We're going to drive out of Phoenix, heading toward Colorado, where we'll pick up a jet to take us home. We'll stop in about 4 hours and bunk in a hotel for the night. I'm booking it now."

"Where's your home? Where do you guys live?" Her hands are fumbling in her lap and I feel an overwhelming urge to pull her onto my lap, cradle her, and protect her.

"New Jersey. I have an apartment there that you both can stay in," I respond, banishing the soft thoughts from my mind.

Lily nods. "Thank you. I really didn't have a clue about any of this. You have to know that."

I believe her. There's no way in hell anyone could put on a performance as good as that. The poor woman is a wreck.

We drive in silence for a good hour before I glance at Reece. His head is mushed against the window and his eyes are shut. His breathing is soft. I decide now may be as good a time as any to talk to Lily. She must read my mind because she speaks up first. "He's not asleep if that's what you're thinking," she says, side-eyeing me with a smug smirk.

I frown and glance back at Reece again. "Looks it to me..."

"Looks can be very deceiving, Cal, and I can assure you that's one of Reece's main traits."

I scoff. The kid is out for the count. I look at him again. Yeah, the kid is definitely asleep. He's peacefully grunting.

"How old is he? What the fuck happened, Lily?" I ask, trying to keep my tone low but annoyance running through it all the same.

She sits a little straighter, rubbing her hands in her lap and looking down at them and back up again. I know my brothers can hear all this but whatever, we needed to talk.

"He's fourteen. He never mentioned trying to find you, Cal. Not once." She exhales and leans her head back against the headrest, exposing her beautiful neck.

"Honestly, I wouldn't even know where to start. I left Vegas the day you left and didn't return. I wasn't about to stick around, Cal, not after what you did. That was my chance to go and make a fresh start. I wanted my degree and I was going to get it..."

My eyebrows raise in confusion. What the fuck did she mean "not after what I did?" I didn't do fuck all.

"Did you get my details, Lily? I left them with reception and they assured me they'd pass the details on."

She laughs sarcastically. "Of course you did. You know, I really am past giving a toss about whether you tried to contact me or not." She shrugs.

"What the hell is that supposed to mean?"

"Cal, I woke up to a note saying 'be back shortly' and a fucking envelope with $10,000. Low and behold, no Cal returned, and no I didn't get any fucking details. But I sure as hell am certain you know that already, so please spare me the 'I tried' part because like I said, I'm past giving a toss. You treated me like a fucking whore and I guess I deserved that."

Wow! Just fucking wow. I go over what she just spat out but that was not how it went down, not at all. Not how I meant it to go down at least...

I'd forgotten about the money. I'd won it on the tables earlier in the night and left it on the dresser when I walked in. I had to leave quickly, so I left the note there next to it.

I don't know if I did...Okay, so I can see why she might have thought I paid her off...Shit, fuck. Had she thought that all this time? I paid her and left? She must have fucking hated me. I was kicking myself internally. What a fucking idiot!

"Lily, I swear to you..." She turns her head away from me. I ball my fists in frustration, because, fuck! I need to make her understand.

My tone deepens with my temper, "Look at me please, Lily. I swear to you that was never my intention. I got a business call. I had to leave. I didn't want to wake you—we had a late night, right? I thought it was best for me to leave a note. I'd left my winnings and didn't even consider them until you just mentioned them. I didn't expect to be long. As soon as I realized I was going to be, I left my details with the reception, and they assured me they would pass my information onto you."

I exhale sharply, desperate for her to hear all the words I'm saying, emotion evident in my voice. "When I didn't hear from you, Lily, I came back to Vegas the following week. I enquired at the bar and they said you'd left, and they'd not heard from you. I asked your colleagues, they said you'd moved on to start college. I fucking hired a PI for fuck's sake.

I spent six years—six fucking years. I've gone back to that bar countless times to try and find you." I take a deep breath. She has to believe me! "Lily, I can look you in the fucking eye and tell you I tried to find you, I wasn't going to let you go. I made you a promise and I was going to keep it."

Reece leans forward and almost throws himself over the seats between me and Lily, scaring the shit of me in the process, the kid was meant to be asleep for fuck's sake!

"He's telling the truth, Mom," he declares.

"Are you sure?" she asks, narrowing her eyes at him.

"Yeah, I'm sure!"

I look at Lily. What the fuck was he talking about? She clears her throat and dips her head slightly, "Reece has learned to study body language. I encouraged it because I thought it would help him to assess situations and make him comfortable in social areas. He's erm... well he's exceeded my expectations, to say the least. He can read people now as well as social situations."

You're fucking kidding me. The kid can read people? Like literally read people like they're fucking books? He's goddamn ingenious!

Oscar chuckles to himself, but more of a disbelief chuckle. I mean, let's face it, he had the top spot in our family for being some weird socially awkward hacker genius and now a kid has come along and wiped him well and truly off that spot. Yeah, he's got some tough competition.

LILY

I relax when Reece sits back. I look out the window, trying to process everything Cal has just told me. All along I thought he'd tried to pay me off. All along I thought his promises were lies. If only I'd stayed another night or received his contact details, maybe everything would have been so much different. So much easier...

I have to put a stop to these emotions and quick, shake myself off and not look back. Looking back got me nowhere and I'm not prepared to go there again.

"Mom, we forgot about my goldfish." The panic in his voice is evident. I take a deep breath and look out the window more deeply. The only way I'm going to get my lie past Reece is to avoid his face at all costs and keep my tone as neutral as possible. "It's okay honey, I sent Mrs. Grainger a text before we left. She's going to take care of them."

"Oh, okay," he replies and I think I might have just gotten away with it. I glance at Cal and he's looking at me with a knowing look. A small discreet smile graces his lips. Yeah, some lies only we adults can tell. He got it.

I take a minute to study him. He looks older but still as gorgeous as before. His skin is darker, almost olive. He has his hair shorter but you can still see the long waves on top. His jaw looks sharper but I'm not sure if it's the stress of the situation.

He's still in good shape. His white shirt is tight across his shoulders and I can tell he still has muscle, if not more. God, he really is fucking edible. No wonder I fell for him. I want to straddle his lap and rip his shirt open, trail my tongue over his fucking pecks while grinding on his dick.

Yeah, well done, Lily. Jump the poor guy's bones after dropping the biggest bombshell of his life on him.

He chuckles at me and his eyes meet mine in jest. Shit, I hadn't realized how long I must have been staring and eye fucking him. I quickly glance away, my cheeks heating.

We are over halfway there and we've had short bursts of conversation about random rubbish, but it has slowly been helping ease my anxiety.

"So, Cal, do I have any siblings? Are you married?" Reece's sudden questions pique my interest. I hadn't thought of that.

Jesus, he could have a whole family back at his home and we were about to ruin it. A rush of nervousness and a strange wave of jealousy wash over me, flooded by a pit of sickness in my stomach.

Cal takes what feels like a lifetime to answer, fucking moron, adding to the suspense.

He's looking between his brothers in front of him, to his hands, and out the window as though he's struggling with the answer. Just fucking tell us already...

"No siblings, Reece. No wife, but I do have a fucking fiancée," he spits it out like it's vitriol.

Bren laughs. "Yep, complete and utter stuck-up bitch that we all hate." Oh, fantastic!

Reece laughs to himself. "Why are you engaged if you don't like her, Cal? I don't understand. I thought you were meant to get married to people that you love." So naïve in some ways. Bless him.

Cal draws his hand down his face. "Yeah, that's never going to happen—the love part, I mean—and if I have anything to do with it the wedding won't happen either. I just need to find a way out of it without it causing too many problems."

My eyebrows shoot up. Wow. What the hell was that supposed to mean?

He obviously took note of my reaction because he goes on to explain. "My father decided I'm much too old at the grand old age of thirty-five to be without a wife and used that as an excuse to tie two family businesses together. Penelope, the fiancée...her family is head of a family we've previously had problems with, a little competition on the sales side of things. Da decided to make a deal with her father and lucky me, I'm the sacrificial lamb to marry her." He speaks with venom but also a defeatist tone. He's clearly had issues with this and it sounds like he'd made his thoughts known, to no avail.

"An arranged marriage? Is that what you're saying?"

"Yeah, that's exactly what it is, Lily. It's not something I can just pull out of. Plans had been implemented before I was even made aware and no fucker is bothered about what I want."

"Do you not like her then?"

He laughs at my question. "Like her? No, I don't fucking like her. She's a pompous pumped up prissy little bitch that's also very fucking happy with Daddy's contract, which needless to say, makes me hate her even more." He's shaking and fuming. Yeah, I've hit a nerve.

"Well, it's going to be fun explaining to Da you've got a kid already to pass his empire on to. Please let me be there when you do," Bren teases.

"Fuck off!" Cal spits.

CHAPTER 5

Lily

We finally reach the hotel. The guys carry the bags to the top floor penthouse and Reece carries Pussy in, tucked under his chin, mumbling away to her. Bren has paid the bellboy to turn a blind eye to the no pets policy.

The room is huge. It has a full living and dining area and three bedrooms, each with an en suite bathroom.

"Which room will Reece want? The one next to yours?" Cal asks as he drops my bag onto the bed. I can smell his cologne. He smells fucking gorgeous.

I scrub my hand down my face to try and snap out of my sudden sexual reawakening.

"He won't go to sleep, Cal. He might nap on the couch. Just leave him and the TV on and he'll be fine."

"What do you mean he won't go to sleep? Every fucker sleeps."

"Yeah, but he struggles with that and just has short

sharp naps. His drugs eventually catch up with him and he'll crash deep within a few days." I shrug.

"A few days?" He blows out, exhaling.

As he leaves the room, he calls, "We're going to order food in from room service. You coming?"

I leave the room to join everyone in the living area. Reece is already on the couch with the TV on and Pussy sitting on his chest. Cal is explaining the sleep issues to Bren and Oscar.

"What do you want to drink, Lily?" Bren asks. He's noticed me standing awkwardly in the entry. He'd spoken to help me relax and engage me.

I already like Oscar. He reminds me of Reece in so many ways. What little Bren has said, and now him pulling me into their close fold, has me softening to him too. They are clearly a tight-knit family and I already love that. I glance at Reece and know he is going to be safe with them. They look out for one another and now he will be a part of that too, something I've never been able to offer him before. It warms me inside.

"A beer would be great, please." The men look at one another and smile. Okay...an inside joke maybe?

CAL

Lily takes the beer. The guys and I are smiling to ourselves. A woman that drinks beer is more on our wavelength than the prissy posh shit that Penelope insists on drinking—fucking outsider. Lily already fits perfectly into our family. I wonder if she realizes it yet. I sit smiling to myself.

I glance down at the menu and pass it to Lily. "So, what would you and Reece like to order, Lily? I'm going to ring it through."

She looks into her lap and then back at me. "Erm, it might be best if I order Reece's burger," she replies, almost shyly.

I can't help but fucking laugh. Was she serious?

"Lily, I can order a fucking burger," I say with a reassuring smile.

She takes another deep exaggerated breath, as though this is hard work.

"Okay, well he has to have it well-done, salad in a side bowl, not on the burger, nothing red in the salad at all, sauces in individual pots on the side, and only a yellow cheese not orange."

What the actual fuck? I look at her, my mouth probably gaping, blinking my uncertainty. Nope, she is not shitting me. She actually wants me to say that shit. She fucking means every word of it. I grab the phone and almost launch it into her chest. "Here you do it. We'll all have burgers, however they fucking come."

I walk toward the fridge. I need something stronger than a beer, ASAP.

Bren stands back and laughs to himself again. Fucking smug comedian bastard. I grab a whiskey and plonk myself on the couch next to Reece. He's completely enthralled with some cartoon shit on the TV. He looks like a normal four-teen-year-old, laughing to himself. That is until I realize there is absolutely no sound coming from the TV and the subtitles on the screen are in Italian. What the hell? I do a double-take at him and the TV.

I look at him blankly. "Reece, buddy, do you understand Italian?"

He spins around and looks at me as though I have two heads. "Yeah, of course I do!"

Then he looks back at the TV, tutting at me for inter-rupting him. I drag my hand through my hair. What the actual fuck?

Lily puts the phone down and lets us know dinner will be about 20 minutes.

"Lily, is Reece fluent in Italian?" Oscar asks. He's been sitting on a dining chair overlooking the couch, watching Reece with curiosity.

She fidgets, doing her signature glance down before replying. "Yeah, he is. He's fluent in four languages, I think."

Bren releases a chuckle. "Jesus, Cal, he's an absolute fucking genius!"

"Yeah, that's not always a good thing," Oscar responds sharply.

"How so?" I want to know my brother's logic. I knew he was intrigued and excited by Reece but what was this apprehension?

Lily answers softly before Oscar can get the chance. "Because he can either be an asset or a liability, depending on whose hands he's in."

My stomach rolls. I look at the kid next to me, in his shorts and T-shirt laughing away to fuck knows what. Yeah, he was a genius, but in the wrong hands? That was not a good thing and no fucking good would come out of it.

We are going to protect him. He is mine and Lily's. He's family and family comes first.

I look at Lily, hoping she can see the trust and honesty behind my words. "Don't worry, Lily. We'll protect him. All of us." I gesture to my brothers, who both nod their heads without hesitation. No fucker is going to touch my family. No fucking one.

LILY

We demolish the burgers. Cal keeps glancing my way and then he looks away just as quick. Bren doesn't make any attempt to look away and to be honest, he is intrigued and isn't afraid to make it known. "You realize Da is gonna want a DNA test done, don't you, Cal?"

Cal spins around and narrows his eyes. "Not needed," he replies, firmly holding Bren's eyes.

"Cal, it's fine. I completely understand why your family needs it all official. It's not a problem. Sort it as soon as we get to your place, please." I look at him reassuringly. He meets my eyes and nods.

I drop my plate onto the tray, glance at Reece, and announce, "I'm off to bed. You going to be okay, honey?"

Reece jumps up. "Oh, Mom, I've got you something." He pulls a black T-shirt from his backpack and I know instantly it's one of Greg's. I smile and pull him into a hug. Reece does have his moments, his thoughtful moments that outweigh his dumb actions tenfold.

He's brought one of Greg's T-shirts with him because

he's remembered the one-off comment I'd once made. "I sleep better in your tee, Greg. Makes me feel safe."

CAL

I'm intrigued about what Reece has pulled from his bag to give to Lily with what was obviously an emotional reaction. A black T-shirt?

"What's that all about?" Bren asks, waving his hand in Lily's direction. Yeah, my brother's watching too.

"Oh, it's Greg's T-shirt. Her fuck buddy. She sleeps better in them apparently," Reece explains, shrugging.

"Redcars, Reece," she snaps, sternly glaring at him.

All our mouths drop open, all of us. Except for Reece, of course, who is now back to sitting on the couch watching subtitles.

Lily's eyes have popped out of her head and they are darting around the room to make a quick exit.

"What the fuck's redcars all about then?" Bren asks.

Lily exhales. "It's a phrase we use when Reece is saying something that you don't want him to continue with, like a safe word, a shut-the-fuck-up-you're-going-too-far word."

"Like a no?" Bren asks again on a chuckle, bemused.

"Yes, Bren, like a hell no, don't-go-there word."

Before anyone can ask anything more...

"Night!" She throws over her shoulder as she leaves the room to go to her bedroom.

I look to Oscar, who shrugs. He's got what now looks like a permanent position watching over Reece with fascination, arms and legs crossed over like a night watchman.

Bren is chuckling and raises his eyebrows when I glare at him. He juts his chin out in the direction of Lily, encouraging me to go after her for a few answers. I nod in agreement.

I walk to Lily's door, knock, and wait.

"Come in." Her sweet voice stirs my cock. I run my hand through my hair. *Fucking calm down, you dick.*

I push open the door and walk in, greeted by her in a long black T-shirt that is almost as far down as her knees, this *fuck buddy* was a big dude. Fucking prick!

That's all she's in, a fucking flimsy T-shirt.

Her hair flows over her shoulders. She swallows as she looks into my eyes, her nipples have pebbled and are visible under her top. Yep, I fucking went there, staring straight down at them.

Jesus, my dick is hard as fuck against my trousers. I've only looked at her for Christ's sake and she's clothed at that.

I clear my throat to break the tension. Yep, sexual tension, because there's no denying that's what this is.

"I, erm, wanted to make sure you're okay?" I ask, rubbing my hand through my hair.

She looks down, then back up to my eyes. "I'll be fine. Thank you, Cal. We'll be fine, I'm sure."

I scratch at my head and tug slightly on my hair, awkward as fuck.

"So, this Greg? Is he your boyfriend or something?" I ask softly. Please say fucking no!

"No, he's not!" she snaps back instantly, clearly not wanting to have this conversation.

"It's just if there's someone in the picture...we need to make sure everyone's safe, Lily. You know Oscar can do shit and tie up loose ends. We need to know if someone might want to find you and Reece. I just want to know who's in your life, to keep you both safe," I softly explain, hoping she doesn't see how pissed off I am that our son has just announced there is a "fuck buddy" whose T-shirt she sleeps in. I mean, if he wasn't someone to her, she wouldn't want to sleep in his fucking top, would she?

She softens her tone and gently explains. "There's no one, Cal. Greg is in the past, like past-past, and he will not be an issue trying to track us down, I can assure you." She gifts me with another one of her beautiful smiles. Her green eyes shine with sincerity.

Well, what can I say to that? I blow a breath out in relief. Thank fuck for that.

I nod to Lily. "I'll leave you to it. Hope you sleep well. We leave at ten in the morning, but no rush. We have a private jet and aren't restricted to departure times so... no rush." Fuck, I don't want to leave her room. Her lips are right there.

"Thank you. Good night, Cal," she says softly as I close the door.

I rest my head back against the door and will myself away from her room. My heart's pounding against my chest. I've finally got her back after all these years of wanting and trying and now she's here with my kid.

I shake my head. What a fucking day.

I walk back to the kitchen area, glancing at Reece, and walk over to my brothers. "We need to give the guys a heads up," Bren states.

"No, I'll tell them. I'll call a family meeting with Ma and

Da. Just get this shit out in the open ASAP. Oscar, can you organize the DNA test?"

"Sure, I mean you don't need it. You only have to look at mini-Cal and you can see, but for Da's sake, I'll sort it. It'll be done tomorrow and may get it back the same day. Maybe the day after."

I nod in agreement and pour myself a Jack D.

Reece is chuckling to himself with the fucking cat still on his chest.

Oscar looks at me. "He's on to Mandarin now."

I look at Oscar in confusion. He nods toward the TV. "Mandarin. The subtitles. He's on to Mandarin now." I blink, then look at Bren, his eyebrows shoot up and he smirks, a smirk I've seen too much of today. I want to knock his fucking smirky head off, cocky shit.

I scrub a hand down my face. "Man, you should go and get some sleep. I'll watch the kid. Whose room are you sleeping in anyway?" Bren jokes, eyebrows dancing.

"Shut the fuck up. Jesus, I've got enough on my plate without you coming out with shit like that."

"Just saying..."

"Yeah well, fucking don't!"

"Is it because she's got a 'fuck buddy?'" The fucking smirking prick laughs. I slam my glass down, ready to fly across the counter.

Reece's head jumps up. "What's wrong?"

I glance at Reece and smile softly. "Uncle Bren making silly jokes. Nothing to worry about."

I glare at Bren and his hands shoot up in defense. "Okay, a little too early for jokes maybe, but this Greg dude, is he going to be a problem?"

I tug on my hair. I can't even stand the prick's name, and "fuck buddy." She has a fucking *fuck buddy*?

"No, I asked Lily and she assures me this prick Greg is history."

"Yeah, that's good news. We've got a shitstorm ahead of us and we don't want any more clusters or casualties along the way. We need to sit down tomorrow and talk shit through with Lily, find out what sort of trouble she's had," Oscar declares.

My head shoots up from my glass. Trouble?

"What trouble? What do you mean? You mean the cartel? You just pin that shit somewhere else, right? Is that what you mean?" My voice panics as my mind struggles to piece things together. My head is already pounding, my mind whirling with all the revelations. Now what?

"That's already done. I changed the usernames on the accounts and sent them on a wild goose chase. It'll take them a long while, if not forever, to link that shit back to us and Reece. But Lily mentioned she'd had problems with the cartel before. That's the shit I'm talking about."

My stomach drops. "When did she say that?"

Bren tuts at me. "Jesus man, were you in the room today? When the kid tried giving her the Valium and she about collapsed at the mention of the cartel, said something like 'can't do the cartel again.'"

I keep my voice low and stern. "No, I don't fucking remember that part of the conversation. I'm still reeling from seeing the girl I pined after for fifteen years. Let alone the whole I've got a kid thing, not to mention he's some fucking genius, whiz, or whatever bullshit you want to call it. So no, I'm fucking sorry I missed the bit where my family has had dealings with the fucking cartel before," I snipe back.

Bren slaps me on the back and lowers his head. "Of course. I'm sorry brother, it's a shit ton to take in. I get it,

Oscar's right. Tomorrow back at your place, we sit down and have a chat with Lily."

I feel relieved that someone else, my brothers particularly, is taking charge and helping handle this shit storm. Tomorrow's a new day and with the feeling in the pit of my stomach, I know it's going to bring more turmoil and revelations. Fuck. My. Life.

CHAPTER 6

Lily

I'd been woken this morning to a soft knock on the door by Oscar, followed by Reece pushing past him and marching into the room with Pussy. They declared breakfast had been ordered and would be there shortly.

Once we'd had a polite breakfast together, we gathered our belongings and made our way to the O'Connells' private jet. Yes, O'Connell was Cal's surname—a name I'd spent many years wishing I'd asked. At the time, Cal had insisted on saving our truths for the next day...the next day that never came.

We'd both wished we'd insisted on having those conversations the one and only night we'd spent together but we never did.

Reece had been well behaved on the jet. He wore his AirPods and Puss was allowed to sit with him. Although he constantly tugged at his hair, he was a lot better than I'd expected. He wasn't a novice to flying privately. Years ago we'd been fortunate enough to have these experiences, but I was still overwhelmed by the enormity of wealth the O'Connell family appeared to have.

I sigh as we pull into the apartment block—a tall modern glass skyscraper that Cal has explained his family built and owned. He and Oscar lived in this one and Bren, Finn, and Connor lived in an identical one on the other side of town.

The underground parking is ultramodern and light, not your typical garage. The lights come on as we enter and illuminate the whole floor.

"This is our private parking. All the vehicles here belong to us. Only cars registered to us are able to gain access," Cal explains as I look through the window.

Dozens of cars line the garage, all sizes, all makes and models.

Jesus, how many cars can you drive for god's sake? I shake my head and look to Reece, who is in awe and giddy with excitement. Cal looks at him and smiles, a big genuine smile. He looks as excited as Reece. It warms my heart.

Entering the elevator, Oscar spends time explaining the security system to Reece, who is lapping up the information. He explains the access codes, handprint system, twenty-four-hour surveillance, fingerprint recognition, and eye scanning software that are used.

I wasn't sure whether to be impressed or concerned that they needed all this. Cal must have picked up on something from my body language or face because he explains, waving his hands around, "It's Oscar's baby—all this IT mumbo jumbo. He likes to be the most up-to-date and most modern in all areas. Nothing to worry about. This is all to help you relax, help all of us relax, not to cause any concern."

I look at him. He looks sincere, reassuring me with a

smile, but I'm unsure if he's trying to convince me or him. Or was Cal just as unaware of anything to be concerned about? I smile to thank him for explaining but deep down I'm not so sure we aren't leaping from the frying pan into the fire, so to speak.

The elevator door opens into the center of the apartment. It's...wow!

Modern, chic, open, and huge.

Dark wood floors throughout, pedestals with glass art stand on either side of the entrance area— that's the first issue right there. Cal is already looking at me for a reaction with excitable hopeful eyes, his teeth tugging at his lower lip. Unfortunately, I'm about to burst his happy bubble.

I drop my bag and sigh. "Shit, Cal, this is too much. Like really too much. These things..." I gesture to the glass art. They look like twisted pieces of metal made from glass. Somebody thought it was worth buying but what the fuck was it meant to be?

"Those right there, anything remotely like that, or remotely as expensive as it looks, shift it *ASAP*!" As I say those words, emphasizing the ASAP part, we hear *smash* just down the corridor to my left. Fuck, here we go!

I hesitantly look at Reece and a thousand shards of glass. "What was it supposed to be?" he asks without an apology. My eyes burst from my sockets. Oh, shit. We haven't been in this place two freaking minutes and shit is already getting trashed. I'm completely panicked and look wide-eyed to Cal, shaking my head. "I'm so sorry, Cal. I was just about to explain, Reece is a little inquisitive and a lot clumsy. Anything of value, please can you find somewhere else for it?"

CAL

I heard it before I saw it and I knew instantly it was the Gwen Damsen $40,000 glass balloons artwork, obliterated in sixty seconds flat. I look down at my shoes and steady my breathing, glancing back up to the most beautiful and nervous eyes I've ever seen.

Lily explains Reece's inquisitive clumsiness. How can I be mad with that? I quickly scan the room and realize my whole damn apartment is full of expensive artwork that needs to be relocated as soon as possible and panic rushes through me. I look to Oscar, who's already tapping away on his tablet frantically.

"Sorted," he announces proudly.

Thank fuck my brother is so efficient. He gets stuff done without us having to ask. I nod to him in appreciation.

"Who buys shit like that anyway?" Reece asks, sauntering around the apartment.

Bren clears his throat. "Clearly your dad buys that shit, Reece. Seeing you're standing in his apartment, everything in here is shit he's bought," he explains while swooping his hand around the apartment.

"You live here?" Lily asks, moving farther into the apart-ment, a little too hesitant for my liking but still moving toward the windows.

LILY

The apartment is beautiful, the back is all windows overlooking New Jersey. Huge white couches line the windows facing toward the front of the apartment. A ginormous TV mounted on the wall is the hub of the living area.

To the right is a kitchen, modern and stylish, white top to bottom, with a breakfast bar. On the other side is a glass dining table for eight people. To both my right and left are corridors that I can only assume lead to bedrooms.

"I do normally live here, but I'll stay downstairs with Oscar in his apartment if you prefer," Cal says while rubbing his hair.

Oscar raises his eyebrows. It's obviously news to him. He just as quickly lowers them and smiles at me with a small polite nod.

Bren is helping clean up the glass and trying to get Reece not to let Puss out of the cage just yet.

"You don't have to move out on my account. Do you have a spare room I could use?"

Cal wanders over to the kettle, filling it with water while gesturing to the couches. "Sure. If you're comfortable with that we'll do that Lily. Please make yourself at home, both of you." He looks toward Reece.

Reece is now wandering around the apartment tugging his hair, clearly desperate for Puss to be let out for him to nuzzle. He begins inspecting things as he walks around, making me cringe internally. Lifting jar lids, pressing buttons in the kitchen. I'm on the edge of the couch, looking down at my hands and back up at Reece. I just want to go to him and sit him down, get him to stop touching and pressing and fucking things up.

But this is Reece and I can't do that. Oscar senses my anxiety and sits next to me. "Don't worry, Lily. Let him explore a little. If he fucks things up, Cal can sort it. Seriously, don't worry!" Oscar is soft and reassuring. He has deep blue eyes that don't jump out like Cal's, they're more subtle. He has a calm and reassuring presence about him.

Cal speaks up, "Lily, do you want coffee?"

"Yes, please. Milk, no sugar."

"I've got some Coke. Will Reece drink that?"

I jump up from the couch. "God no. Jesus Cal, don't give him Coke, like ever never give him Coke!"

Bren laughs. "We do mean the drink Coke, Lily. Coca-Cola. We're on the same page, right?"

My head shoots back toward Bren. "Yes, smart ass, I know perfectly well your brother means the drink. What I mean is, if you want an absolute shit-storming riot to begin in your brother's apartment, followed by an absolute fuel fucked-up tantrum, do please give him a Coke..." I wave my hand to the Coke can.

"O-kay then. Maybe a glass of water?" Cal laughs gently.

I laugh softly and everyone else follows, the tension soon eased. I like that we can go from zero to a thousand and within seconds I'm calm again and the atmosphere light. I'm loving this feeling of sharing my anxiety and the pressure. I never thought I'd get to share any of it.

We're sitting at the glass table with our drinks, watching Reece take in his surroundings. He's happier and more settled now that Puss can come out.

Oscar has somehow arranged for staff to collect Cal's art structure things and put them somewhere safe out of the apartment.

I'm relieved and can start to unwind. Tension slipping away from me, I roll my neck from side to side.

Cal sits straighter and runs his fingers through his hair. This must be an O'Connell trait—Reece does this regularly when he gets nervous too.

"Lily, we need to talk about a few things, get some understanding about yours and Reece's past." He gestures to his brothers.

My spine straightens and the tension returns tenfold. I take a gulp and glance at my hands in my lap. I want to be honest with Cal, with his brothers. I'm so fed up carrying the burden of our past and future by myself, but I'm not sure I'm strong enough to deal with the implications of letting them know our history.

"I...I'm not sure where to start," I say honestly. I twist my hands in my lap.

Cal looks to Oscar, who's looking at his tablet. Oscar looks up. "How about I ask you some questions, Lily, and you answer them honestly? Anything you don't want to answer or can't answer with honesty, you just say pass.

"But, Lily, you can and must trust us. Know that, please. We're here for you and have got yours and Reece's best inter-ests at heart and will do everything in our power to help you both, okay?"

CAL

I stare at Oscar. What the fuck was that speech all about?

Bren is glaring at him. He's as intrigued as me. Oscar has found something while tapping away on that tablet of his and now has questions he knows Lily won't be comfortable answering. What the fuck? Was she in trouble? Was she hiding shit?

I look at her and she slowly nods in agreement with Oscar's suggestion. He gives her a soft smile and nods in response.

He starts, "Okay, so I was looking into yours and Reece's background and can't find your names on any records. Mr. Warriner was down as the lease holder on your apartment but no mention of you or Reece. Can you explain that for me?"

She appears nervous as hell, quickly looking up and back down. "There is no Mr. Warriner. Reece used that name as an alias for us." My eyes widen and I listen more intently, trying not to give off any body language that might make her more nervous. I'm pissed at the secrets Lily seems to hold on to. I'm not sure why I feel that way.

"What about the fact that I can't find records for you and Reece? How is that possible?"

My head shoots up at that. What the fuck? Why the fuck didn't they have documentation and how? I look to Oscar for an explanation. He's watching Lily closely, gauging her reaction.

She sits straighter and looks at Oscar. "Pass"

I launch out of my seat. "Bullshit, Lily. What the fuck is going on? How can you not have documentation? How can you both not exist?"

Lily looks around the room quickly, looking for Reece. Thankfully he'd wandered off to explore the bedrooms. She lowers her voice and Bren nods, encouraging me to sit down.

"Oscar said if I wasn't comfortable answering questions, then I didn't have to, so pass." She shrugs with one shoulder.

Bren fidgets in his seat, his jaw tense, also pissed with that response.

"This is my son, Lily. I deserve to fucking know what the hell you guys have been doing for the last fourteen years, where you've been, and what shit you've got yourselves into," I snipe. She gasps at my tone, but I'm furious with her responses, or lack of.

Oscar looks at Lily, analyzing her and gently asking, "Okay. Is this something to do with the comment you made to Reece at the apartment about not being able to deal with the cartel again?" Lily's eyes bug out of her head, her face flushes, her breathing becomes heavier. Bingo!

"Mom." Lily's head shoots around to Reece, glaring daggers at him. We all look toward Reece with bated breath.

"No, Reece. Redcars, Reece. Do you hear me? Redcars, Reece. Redcars," she frantically yells at our son, her chest heaving in panic.

Reece continues to walk forward. "Mom, I think..."

Lily shuts him down quickly, leaping out of her seat and making direct eye contact with him. "No. I said no. Did you hear me? Red. Fucking. Cars!"

Reece shakes his head, tugging on his hair as he falls onto the couch and rocks backward and forward.

"Lily, what the hell's happening? What's this all about?" I ask, waving my hand at Reece, panic evident in my voice. Something big is happening here, something Reece wants to share and Lily doesn't.

"Lily"—Oscar gently coaxes—"you can trust us. I swear we can help keep you safe and support you both." He looks into her eyes and nods gently.

Me? I'm losing my fucking mind, and fast. Bren's breathing deeply, his jaw ticking in frustration, his palms clenching. Yeah, my older brother doesn't handle shit too well unless he can do it with his fists or a weapon. He's quickly losing control.

"Lily, has something happened previously with the cartel that Reece had something to do with?" She slowly looks up from her lap with tears in her eyes. My heart races. She's fucking killing me here. I want to wrap her up and take all the shit away—past, present, and fucking future. I want it all but she needs to let us in.

"There was a bit of trouble a few years ago." She struggles to get her words out, her hands shaking, tears streaming down her face.

The next thing I know, Reece has jumped up, red-faced and breathing heavily, pounding up and down on his feet. Tugging at his hair, he's inconsolable. We all look at him, astonished and unsure how to approach him. "It wasn't all my fault. It wasn't, I swear. I told you it wasn't. Mom, I told you!"

"Reece, stop it. Please, honey, it's okay. It's not your fault. It's fine—done, dusted, doesn't matter. Leave it at that, please. Okay?" She tries to placate him.

Lily gently strokes Reece's shoulder, consoling him, but he's moving away from her, gently pushing her and shaking his head back and forth. I flick toward Oscar, whose eyebrows are furrowed. He shrugs with a desperate look on his face. He clearly suspected something like this, something big.

Bren's back is ramrod straight.

Me? I feel sick and just want to know what the fuck is happening. And how the fuck I can help my son. I'm useless at the minute and it kills me to admit it.

"It was your fucking boyfriend that caused it all, not me," Reece declares.

Lily gasps, holding her hand to her mouth. "Shut the fuck up, Reece, right now. Redcars right now, Reece," she screeches, her face full of anguish and despair.

I stand. This is getting out of fucking control. We need to know what this shit is about and what the hell is happening.

"Reece, what the fuck are you talking about, buddy?" I try coaxing it out of him as gently as I can when I want to fucking scream, tell me what the fuck is going on!

"I heard them talking and he was saying shit about my mom, so I thought I'd teach him a fucking lesson." He throws himself on the couch in a ball, screeching and tugging his hair. He evidently didn't want to hold back but was having an internal struggle for his mom's sake. She plainly thought it was necessary to hold back.

I turn to Lily. "Lily, baby, you need to sit down and talk to us. We've got you. You can tell us any fucking thing but you do need to tell us. Look at Reece. He needs you to tell us." I stroke her face gently and lower my voice. "We're here for you. You can trust us. You can trust me," I plead.

She finally nods. With a sharp intake of breath, she falls to the couch, breathing out and looking down at her feet. She straightens her back and looks up at me with regained composure. "I had a relationship with someone when Reece was seven. I later found out his family was part of the cartel." She licks her lips and looks down at her hands, then back up to me. My eyes scrutinize her face and carefully chosen words.

"We were together a few years. The relationship didn't end good. The man's father didn't approve and Reece heard some things and decided to wreak a little revenge. The revenge ended the relationship, I moved on, and for obvious reasons decided it was best to keep our heads down." She lets it out and I try to take it all in. She's given us the basics, carefully crafted basics. But at least it's something, right?

I look to Oscar, who's watching Lily with laser eyes. He's already taken onboard her words and is about to get what he really wants, answers.

"Who was the man you were in a relationship with, Lily? The family name too, please," Oscar asks sternly, not giving her room to maneuver.

I take a hold of her hands in front of me. I'm on my knees and holding her hands for support. I nod at Lily to encourage her. She looks back up at me and my stomach drops. I can see it in her eyes—the pain, the trauma.

She looks at me with intensity and her eyes quickly dart away. "Nico Garcia."

I drop her hands and stumble backward, my heart wrenched from my chest. Bren jumps out of his chair and Oscar drops his head in his hands and pulls his hands down his face.

Nico. Nico fucking Garcia. Is she fucking serious? The Garcias? They're fucking lunatics, the lot of them.

"Jesus fucking Christ, Lily, you were in a relationship with Nico Garcia? The fucking Nico Garcia? Are you out of your damn mind?" I shout.

"She was going to marry him too!" Reece chimes in. He's been quiet these past few minutes and I'd forgotten about his little outburst. This is his latest cluster fuck.

I walk away, pacing up and down, breathing heavily. I take deep breaths with my hands on my hips, trying to calm myself. I brush my hands through my hair. Fuck, fuck, fuck!

Reece's words run through my mind again. I spin on my heel. "You were going to marry him?"

"Yes," she squeaks.

"As in, you loved him, going to marry him?" I shout at her, clear disgust dripping from my mouth.

"Yes, Cal, loved him going to marry him. What a stupid fucking question," she snipes back.

That knocks me back on my feet. She fucking loved him? A fucking cartel? A Garcia? She was going to marry a fucking Garcia and bring my son up with him! I can't look at her. Bren passes me a glass of Jack D and I down the fucker in one.

I look up to Reece. He's sitting up now and you wouldn't know he's had an outburst.

I stare down at Lily. I'm fucking seething, but she's sitting with her knees tucked up to her chest and tears streaming down her face. She looks lost, broken. Fuck, she kills me. What the fuck is wrong with me?

I go over to her and bend down. I needed to know... I can barely get the words out. "Do you still love him?"

She looks up at me with hatred in her eyes. "No!" She's

firm about it, that's for sure. There's no doubt in my mind she means that.

Thank fuck! I can work with that, thank fuck. I relax.

"She doesn't love him anymore. Not since he killed their baby," Reece declares. All our heads spin to Reece. He's stroking Puss and is very nonchalant about his latest comment. I look back to Lily. Her eyes are shut tight, blocking out his words.

"He killed your baby?" I ask gently.

Slowly Lily opens her eyes, struggling to keep composure and nods. "Yes, he did."

"Fuck," Bren says, dropping back into his seat.

"How did he do that Lily?" I ask, gently taking her hands into mine. I rub reassuring circles over her thumbs.

"He stabbed her in the stomach to get rid of the baby." Our eyes dart to Reece in shock.

"Reece, dude, seriously, shut the fuck up!" Oscar snaps.

Reece is taken aback. He hasn't seen this side of Oscar. Yep, this side was my brother alright. He takes so much and then *boom*.

"Look, I think Lily and Reece have been through enough tonight. Why don't we get them settled and we can talk again tomorrow or whenever. Oscar wants to sort the DNA shit out and then we can go to Dad with the results tomorrow," Bren suggests.

I look at Lily. She's dumbstruck. "Yeah, man, that's a good idea. Oscar, get this DNA shit done while I show Lily her room and then I'll settle Reece." He nods in response.

"Come on, Lily, let me show you to your room." I hold out my hand and she takes it. Her hand feels tiny in mine, soft and gentle just like her. I want to wrap her up and never let her go. I walk her down the corridor to the right. I know exactly where she's sleeping.

LILY

Cal guides me down the corridor to the first door on the right. He opens it and pulls me in. I look around in awe. My eyes are still stinging and sore from the tears I'd hoped I'd never shed again.

The room is bright and airy with windows top to bottom, a beautiful gray sleigh bed and soft gray linen, white carpets and white furnishings. It's decorated beautifully and so spacious, it has a calming feel to it.

"The bathroom and walk-in closet are through there." Cal gestures with his hand to the left. I follow and I'm dumbstruck by the most elegant bathroom I've ever seen. It's white and gold, with a huge roll-top bath that looks big enough for a family and an enormous shower with multiple shower heads. Countertops line the wall with mirrors above and gold his and hers sinks. At the opening to the bathroom is another door. "Closet," Cal explains.

He clears his throat. "I'm going to order food in. Any preference?"

"Chinese, Italian, anything really. Thank you," I reply quietly with a shrug.

He smiles. "No Coke, right?" He laughs gently, trying to lighten the mood.

"Right." I smile back.

Cal fidgets on the spot, his hand rigorously moving through his hair. "Well, you shower up or whatever. I'll leave your bag on the bed. Dinner should be about an hour. I'll get the guys out and we can settle Reece down, okay?"

I nod in response. "That's great. Thank you, Cal."

He turns and leaves the room, gently closing the door.

CAL

"DNA all done, man. Should be back at 10:00 a.m. tomorrow. I've called Da and told him we need a family meeting tomorrow at 11:00 sharp."

"Thanks, Oscar. I appreciate it. Both of you, thank you for today." I nod toward them both with a deep exhale.

"Reece is down the corridor on the left. He's been trying to figure out how to get in the den," Oscar says with raised eyebrows, cringing.

Fucking Jesus. I drag my hand over my face. "That gonna be a problem?"

Oscar laughs confidently. "No fucking way. He won't get in there."

"Good. That's the last thing we need! We need to rein this shit in with him. Clearly things have gotten out of control." They both nod in agreement.

"We need to talk shit through with Lily some more, man. Nico Garcia? Seriously? I mean, we need to find out what happened," Bren states the fucking obvious with a clenched fist.

"Yeah, I know, and we will, but enough for today. I'm not

sure how much more we can all take." They both sigh in agreement.

"Anyway, best go and see how my kid is, eh? Make sure he's not trashed anymore priceless fucking shit?"

"Yeah, we'll see ourselves out. Night, man."

"Night," we call to one another.

I walk down the corridor, the one opposite Lily's room—my old room. I smile to myself. I may have been a little bit crafty letting Lily have the master suite and encouraging Reece to choose one from this side of the apartment, but I'm thinking long-term.

I walk into the bedroom next to the den and see Reece on the king bed with Pussy crawling over him.

"Hey man, you chose this room?"

"Yep. Is that wall bombproof?" he asks, pointing to the adjacent wall between his room and the den. What the fuck? Bombproof?

"Erm, I'm sure it is. Yes, man." Jesus, did he think he was going to blow through the fucking wall?

"You don't sound very sure and your Adam's apple is going. Are you lying right now?"

"Jesus Reece, you just asked if a wall in my apartment is bombproof. Made me a bit nervous that's all. Don't bring no bombs in here, okay? I can't be dealing with shit like that. The room is bombproof. Oscar would have made sure of it," I snipe while rubbing my hair.

"Mmm," he replies, sounding unconvinced.

"So, if you want to change the colors in the room, we can arrange it. Or if you want to add anything or take anything down."

He looks around. "Yeah, this isn't going to do, Cal. I need a bigger room for me and Puss." He points to the cat. Is he fucking kidding me? The room is spot on. It has a king bed with side tables, walk-in closet, and a good size en suite bathroom. He's come from a shitty apartment and I doubt it even housed a king bed.

"What were you thinking then, Reece?" I ask coolly.

"Well, I'm gonna need a new gaming and computer area and somewhere decent to sit. Oh, and somewhere relaxing to do my homework. Pussy could do with some scratching posts and shit so I think it's best to knock through into the room next door."

I fucking choke. He wants to redesign the fucking apartment so the cat can have a fucking scratching post? Is he for real?

I clear my throat and decide to change the subject. "Do you need some help putting your clothes away?"

He throws his arm toward the suitcase. "Yeah, they're all in there." Okay, looks like I'm doing it... I take a deep breath and start unpacking his things.

Reece starts flicking through the TV channels nonchalantly.

I have a thought... Smiling to myself, I quickly glance at the door while Lily is busy. I decide to do a little light digging.

"So, this Greg dude, your mom's friend, you like him?" I ask breezily.

He narrows his eyes at me, surveying me. Yep, the little shit is sharp. "He was her fuck buddy, but he was both our friends, not just Mom's. Mine too and I trust him. So yeah, I like him," he replies with a knowing smirk.

Little punk, that hit deep—his *trust him* statement.

"Well, I'm your dad, Reece, so you can trust me too. And your uncles, you can trust them, all of us. We're your family. Yours and your mom's."

"Mmm, I've heard that shit before. Nico said we could

trust him and he tried to kill my mom and the baby, so I reserve judgment just yet on who to trust, thank you very much," he says with a smug ass grin. He got that fucker from his Uncle Bren. I want to knock it right the fuck off.

There's an awkward silence between us as he continues to flick through the TV channels, tutting at the choices available.

"So, what's this Greg do to earn your trust then?" I stop and look at him while holding his tops on a hanger.

"He saved us, me and my mom. We'd be dead without his help. Then he taught me shit to help keep us safe so... he earned my trust and my mom's," he says with a shrug as though it was nothing. More questions whirl in my head but I need to coax them gently and earn some trust myself, they'd obviously been fucked over and I needed them both to feel safe and secure with me.

"Have you got anything Puss can have for dinner?"

I close the drawers. "Yeah, we can find something in the fridge. Come on, buddy."

LILY

I've just had the best shower ever. I've unpacked my clothes and while doing so, discovered that this room was more than likely the master and it belongs to Cal. His clothes are hanging in the closet and his belongings scattered around the room. I may have sniffed his shirts like a weirdo but his scent makes me feel safe as well as horny. I mean, the man is still a walking sex god.

I discover a box of unopened condoms in his bedside drawer and a sinking feeling deep in my stomach overwhelms me. Was he having sex with Penelope? Was the arrangement between them more than just business? Maybe casual sex and a business arrangement?

My hands fumble with the drawer as I shut it closed.

I take a deep breath and close my eyes. I can do this. I need to stay on track, keep me and Reece safe, and find out Cal's true intentions.

I pull on my cardigan and make my way to the kitchen. I can hear Cal and Reece laughing at something. I feel myself get excited inside. This is what it should be like—a family together. This is what I want. I just hope Cal wants it too.

CAL

I see Lily approach out of the corner of my eye. Her hair is in a messy bun and she has short PJs on, a camisole trimmed in lace, and a long gray cardigan over the top. She takes my breath away. So stunning.

She looks beautiful. Her legs are golden—yep, those fuckers need wrapping around my neck. Her stomach is flat, hips wide enough to hold onto. I slowly work my gaze up her body. Her fucking nipples are pebbled again and her tits are full, making her camisole tight at the top. I want to follow that lace with my tongue and dip into her top, rip her tits out, and suck her fucking nipples. Her neck is delicate. My hand would look so good around it. Her lips are full and I close my eyes imagining them around my cock.

I open my eyes and look into her big green eyes looking back. With a knowing smirk, she darts out her tongue and trails it over her lower lip seductively. "You boys having fun?"

I glance away quickly. After getting busted eye fucking her, I shift my attention back to Reece and move behind the counter so she can't see my rock-hard cock.

Clearing my throat I reply, "We were just making our way through the fridge to see what Pussy likes to eat."

"You were looking for Pussy to eat?" She grins. My eyes dart to her standing there laughing silently to herself. I narrow my eyes at her with a knowing look.

"Pussy likes anything fishy. Mom, Cal said he'd order whatever fish I want, but tonight Puss is eating cream. Aren't you, Puss Puss?" Reece's tone is childlike while speaking to his cat.

I glance up at Lily smirking. "Yes, Lily, tonight Puss is eating cream and tomorrow Puss may smell a bit fishy, but it'll be worth it." She quickly covers her mouth with her hand to hide a playful grin.

"So, what's for dinner then, Cal?"

"Do you not want cream, Lily? Is that what you're saying?" Reece narrows his eyes at me. Okay shit, I need to be a bit more subtle with the innuendos.

"Italian you said, Cal. Mom likes Italian." Reece's tone is annoyed. He hasn't seemed to grasp the innuendos, thank fuck.

Lily's eyebrows raise with a small smile on her face. "I'll get the plates."

A few minutes later, the doorbell rings and I go over to the security monitor by the door.

I take the food to the table where Lily and Reece are now sitting.

"Wow, you ordered a lot!"

"Wasn't sure what you'd like so I ordered plenty."

"Did you get chips too?"

"Yeah man, got you those as requested. Both you and your mom need to do me a list for groceries and I'll get the order done. Anything you want." I give Lily a pointed look.

"Thank you, Cal. As soon as I can find work, I'll help out."

I put my fork down. "What do you mean, work? Where would you work?"

She fidgets and avoids my stare. "Well, before all this I worked at a diner, cash in hand of course, due to...you know. And I also volunteered at a lawyer's firm that offered free advice to clients in need of legal help."

"Did you ever start your degree?" I query, raising my eyebrow.

"Yeah, I just have one year left, then I can get my license. But then all this happened with Nico and... yeah, I couldn't finish it, not financially or technically. I was worried he'd trace my name. He knew I wanted the degree so..." She shrugs with a disappointed sigh.

"Nico was paying for Mom's degree. He was good like that," Reece announces.

I almost choke. Good like that? Good like killing his mom's baby?

Lily looks up from her lap to meet my eyes. "Believe it or not, before the incident, he was very good to me and Reece." Of course, he was!

I scoff. Fucking sounds very good. Tried killing his fiancée and baby, sounds like a fucking hero to me. We fall silent as we eat.

I decide to change the subject. "So what do you guys like to do for fun? Do you like sports, Reece?"

He bites into the pizza and takes a handful of chips, shoving them in his mouth. "Nope," he answers with chips spitting from his lips.

Lily smiles beside him. I wonder if she remembers me telling her I hated sports too.

"I like the beach!" Reece says.

"Me too." I nod in agreement.

"Do you like cars?" I ask, remembering his face light up in the garage when we arrived.

"Fuck yeah. Nico let me drive his Ferrari Enzo on the estate when his dad wasn't there, and I was allowed in the classics." Of course, he fucking did and of course, he was allowed in the classics, fucking Nico prick. God, I hate him.

Lily must have seen my unimpressed face and changes the subject again. "So are your family well, Cal? You have five brothers, right?"

Lily's face drops, probably as a direct consequence of mine. I shake my head gently and with my head lowered say, "I erm, I have four brothers now. We lost Keenan about 7 years ago."

"Oh my god, Cal, I'm so sorry. Jesus, that's awful. How's your mom doing?" Her voice is soft and laced with concern.

"She's okay. A lot quieter than she was but she's a strong woman and has Da to keep her on her toes so..." I shrug, unsure what else to say.

Lily smiles at me softly. "I'll save the rest here for tomorrow night." She points down to the food.

"You're going to see your family in the morning. Is that right? With the DNA results?"

"Yeah, Sam, one of the guards, is going to stay here with you guys. I'd prefer it for the time being until things are figured out, and then we can move forward."

She smiles in agreement.

"Do you want to show me your room, Reece?"

"Not really, no," Reece responds while casually eating chips. Lily sighs at his lack of enthusiasm.

"I'll do it. Come on, Lily." I offer my hand and she slips hers into mine as I guide her down the corridor. Her soft warm hand makes my cock stir. That would feel so good wrapped around me.

I clear my throat as we pass the den first. "What's in there?" she asks, pointing to the hand scanner.

"It's where Oscar keeps his computer backup, surveillance cameras, and shit."

"Jesus, don't let Reece in there then." She giggles and I laugh with her. My thoughts exactly.

I point down the corridor, explaining where the spare room, laundry, and the gym are.

"This is Reece's room." I gesture with my hand as I open the door.

Lily walks into the room and turns around on her toes. "Wow, Cal. He's so lucky. He only had a single bed at the apartment and not much room for his tech stuff. Jesus, I bet he's chuffed to bits he's got so much space." Her eyes widen with excitement.

I can't help but drop my head with a shake and laugh to myself, the little shit.

I'm both pleased and proud that Lily is comfortable and impressed with the apartment. It makes me feel something inside, something I hadn't felt capable of in a long time... happiness.

"So, I noticed you gave me the master suite, huh?" Her eyebrows dance in a taunting way, her smirk dancing on her lips.

I scratch my head. "Mmm, you noticed that? What gave it away?" I ask her in jest.

Lily smiles. "Oh you know, the men's products in the bathroom, clothes in the closet, Breitling watches in your dresser, condoms in the bedside table..." My eyebrows shoot up at the last item. Shit.

"Yeah well, all that shit is in there because it's our master suite, Lily, but the condoms are there because that's where they're kept. I've never brought another female back here and don't intend on doing. That's our bed, no fucker else belongs in it." I tuck a strand of hair behind her ear as I lean in closer to make sure she understands exactly what it is I'm saying.

Lily gulps and looks up at me. "What do you want from me, Cal?"

I step back. How could she not fucking know that?

I take her hand in mine. Uncurling her dainty fist, I gently kiss each finger. "Us, Lily. You, me, and Reece. We're going to be a family like we should have fucking been for the last fifteen years. Nothing and no one is going to stop that. Do you hear me?"

She swallows thickly. "You're engaged, Cal, engaged to be fucking married!"

"Yeah, that isn't going to fucking happen!" I snap confidently.

She laughs sarcastically. "Really? You believe that? You expect me to wait around? I'm not going to be a side piece Cal, so don't even remotely think of it. I deserve better than that." She closes her eyes and lowers her head. She's upset and doesn't want me to see. Yeah, fuck that. I want all of her!

"You're right. You do deserve better, you and Reece, and I'm going to give it to you, to both of you. You're not going to be no side piece, Lily. You're going to be my fucking world!" She looks up at me with a lone tear running down her face and she looks so damn fucking beautiful.

"I fucking love you, Lily. I should have said that fifteen years ago. One of the biggest mistakes I ever made. They... my family said I'd get over you..." I shake my head at the dumb memories, the fucking ridicule. "I never got over you and when I saw you in that apartment, you nearly brought me to my knees. I'm never, fucking ever letting you go again. Do you hear me?" She nods gently as I cup her face in my hands.

"Mom! Pussy has shits and it's in the fridge." We both look up and let out a small confused laugh.

"God, I'm so sorry, Cal."

"Seriously, stop apologizing, Lily. He's our son. Ours. We deal with this together. Shit and everything." I laugh while waving my hand in Reece's direction.

I scrub my hand over my hair and smile, opening the door. Little fucking cock blocker that's for sure.

"You go to bed. You look whacked. I'll sort the kitchen and settle Reece, okay?" She nods.

"Mom, before you go to bed, I need a quick word..." I glance over at them both while collecting paper towels for the shit. Reece is looking directly at me while whispering something to Lily. What the fuck?

I try to busy myself to give them space, but I can tell Lily is uncomfortable. Her back is ramrod straight and her shoulders tense. That bugs the shit out of me and pisses me off. What the fuck was being said? Yeah, I'm speaking to Oscar first thing tomorrow. I want to know every fucking thing.

CHAPTER 7

Cal

I don't know how much sleep I fucking got but it wasn't a lot. If I wasn't reliving the past two days over and over, I was thinking of what the fuck Da was going to say today and how the hell I was going to get out of this marriage.

I also had the bonus of Reece unsettled in the living area. The kid seemed determined not to sleep. If he wasn't exploring the apartment for the thousandth time he was eating and watching subtitles while talking to himself or the fucking TV. Apparently, he was digesting the translations. Yeah, mind fucking blown.

I wake properly about 5:00 a.m. with the biggest fucking hard-on, knowing the most beautiful woman I'd ever set eyes on is right next door. While I'm over the fucking moon about that, I'm also feeling fucking anxious she isn't in the same bed as me. Yeah, that needs to change.

I need it cemented. I need her to know for sure that this

is what's happening, and I don't give a flying shit what anyone else thinks about it.

I decide to have a quick shower and tug the fucking beast. I've been so hard it's becoming near on impossible to maintain a safe distance around Lily without wanting to drag her onto my cock. A bit fucking difficult when Reece is around or I'm thinking about Lily's fucking nipples in some other dude's shirt. Yeah, that almost stops the flow, but her nipples outshine that slight stumbling block.

I close my eyes and stand under the showerhead, imagining her green eyes looking at me as her tongue swipes over her lips. I fist my dick harder, squeezing it, imagining Lily's tight pussy clenching it—in and out, in and out. Fuck that feels good.

In my mind I grip her tit and twist it roughly. A moan escapes those sexy greedy lips, desperate to taste my come, desperate for me to fill her holes. I stroke the pre-come down my shaft, rub my balls, and tighten the grip on my cock. As I begin pumping into my hand, my hips jerk with the movement. I slam my hand against the tiled wall as I imagine thrusting into Lily at piston speed. She screams at me to fuck her harder, faster.

I feel the tingling in my balls. I imagine licking those tits and pulling on those nipples. My cock becomes increasingly hard and tight. I rest my thumb on my slit, imagining it hitting that perfect spot inside my woman. She's begging for me to come. I pant as the sensation erupts from my balls up my shaft and rope after rope of thick come coats my stomach as I imagine it coating her pussy.

I wash it down with the showerhead and lean my head back. I need her, a taste of her. I'm prepared to take anything she can give.

I pull on some fresh clothes and walk into the living

room. Reece is crashed out on the couch, face down, the cat beside him. I stop in my tracks. My heart has sped up. My boy is in my living room. This is so fucking crazy. I shake my head with the awareness.

Gently I brush his arm. "Reece buddy, shall we put you to bed?"

He stirs slowly and sloppily. He throws his legs from the couch, appearing drunk. He gets up, stumbling warily, the cat in his arms. As we enter his room, he drops the cat to his bed and pulls his top off, dropping it to the floor in a daze.

His eyes are glazed and red and if I didn't know better, I'd say he's stoned. In a trance, he crawls into bed, mumbling a little louder with each word. "I'm pleased to be here, Dad," he says groggily.

It hits me like a fucking truck, literally taking my breath away. I can't swallow, my throat thickens with emotion. I fucking love this kid. How the hell did that happen so quickly? I wouldn't even say we'd bonded but I feel a magnetic pull, a tug in my gut that shoots through me, and need to protect him.

I pull the covers over him and stroke my hand through the familiar thick dark waves of his hair. "I'm pleased to have you here too, Reece," I say quietly. I know he's asleep but just in case he isn't, I had to say it.

LILY

Cal walks through the doors of the club for the third night in a row, flashing a bright dazzling smile that makes his blue eyes twinkle with mischief. I glance down at the beer I'm pouring, smiling to myself and trying not to be too obvious at how delighted I am to see him again.

As he approaches the bar, I grab a bottle of Corona and plonk it in the space in front of the stool that has become his regular spot.

He's been coming here for months now, and even though I know he's not local and he only came to Vegas for business, I still don't know what he does for a living or his full name. Some would ask if that bothered me. No, why would it? I couldn't judge—I refuse to give him my real name or tell him where I live.

I work in a strip club and we were all given stage names to protect our identities and private lives. Not many people stuck with this club long. It didn't have the best reputation, but the money was good and the tips even better. I only work the bar so it isn't too bad for me, but I know some of the dancers have it rough with clingers and even stalkers. It made me all the more determined to keep my head down, my private life private, and do what I had to do to move on to better things.

Cal is quieter than normal. Over the numerous visits, we'd gotten chatty between the rush and regulars. His first visit was with his brothers, who were celebrating a birthday. Cal hadn't joined in with the usual birthday banter, lap dance, striptease, that sort of thing. Nope, he didn't join in at all. He watched it happen from a distance and kept catching my eye at the bar, then he'd put his head down and smile to himself.

After a couple more visits, he stiffly asked me if I danced here. I choked on my water and when I laughed a "hell no," his shoulders visibly relaxed and he smiled that gorgeous smile that made those blues twinkle more than I thought was possible.

He clears his throat and glances up from his beer. His brown curly hair has fallen over his eyes and I feel the need to brush it away. I am stunned to the spot when he asks, "What time do you get off today?"

He's skirted around asking me out for weeks now. Every time I felt it coming, I was disappointed when it never did. "I finish at five a.m.," I say on a heavy breath.

"So do you fancy going and getting breakfast, you know, instead of the whole dinner thing?" he asks from under his lashes while ripping the wrapper off the beer bottle.

"That'd be great." *Okay, play it cool. That was a little too eager.* I laugh a little and put my head down, embarrassed.

"Well, I'm going to head back to the hotel, try my luck at

the casino, but I'll be here just before five, okay?" he says, standing.

"Sure," I nod coyly, biting my lip.

Cal is true to his word. He arrives on time and drives us to a small restaurant just off the main strip. I'd changed at work because there was no way in hell I ever left that joint in a pair of booty shorts and a cropped top that barely covered my tits.

We order breakfast and the silence is uncomfortable. Cal is nervous and keeps pushing his hands through his hair. I decide to help him out. "How long are you in the city for?"

"Tomorrow's my last night before I head home." Again he goes quiet.

"Do you have far to travel?" He looks down and winces, then looks back at me. I feel like I'm melting under his gaze.

He clears his throat and straightens his back, feigning confidence. "Yeah, I'm from the East Coast, so that's why I never stay long when I come here." He looks at me for a response.

"Are your brothers in town?"

"No, they're busy with work and stuff. Do you have any siblings?" he asks, quickly changing the subject from why he's actually in town.

"Nope. Lucky me, I'm an only child," I reply sarcastically. "When I have kids, I need more than one. It's very lonely."

"Well, you'd love growing up in my house. It's anything but lonely. I crave being left the fuck alone. I've got five brothers and an overbearing father that has all our lives mapped out and no alternative option."

"Wow, I take it you're in a family business then?"

"Yep, never wanted to but hey ho, what the old man says goes. My older brother was a legend in school at football—

like the NFL was working with colleges to offer him placements. Yeah, my Da soon put a stop to that, withdrew him from school so he could "get his head out of the clouds and concentrate on what really mattered, like the family business." "Course I was the disappointment, the son that was never into any sports, but it never did Bren any favors so..." He shrugs.

"Sounds like an ass." I laugh, trying to lighten the mood. Luckily, he laughs at that too, thank god.

"Yeah, he is an ass. A complete ass." He grins.

"Me and my brothers are convinced my mom wanted a girl. There's quite an age gap between me and my younger three brothers. We know my Ma had numerous miscarriages and me and Bren remember her being pregnant, far enough along to have a bump, but she never had the baby. It's not something we talk about, but she's got this sadness in her eyes, ya know." I nod at Cal's openness.

"I'm very close to my Uncle Don. He's everything my father isn't—patient, supportive, proud. My Uncle played a major part in our childhoods. He was the 'fun guy.' He would take us to his cabin every summer and we'd do the same things other kids do. You know... fishing, swimming in the lake, that sort of thing. It gave us a break from the pressures we had at home, he made us feel normal." He clears his throat. "I'd like you to meet him. He'd love you, I know that." He smiles.

I smile back at him. "I'd like that too, Cal." He beams a mega-watt smile at me. He wants me to meet his family? This is amazing.

"So, what about your parents?" Cal enquires after a few minutes.

"Well, my mum is dead and my alcoholic dad's a prick. He's a 'whore yourself out and make some real money' kind of ass," I take on my father's gruff tone, mimicking him.

Cal chokes on his coffee. "Your dad suggested that?" he asks, his eyes wide with shock.

"Yep, I know right? Who the hell wants their one and only child to whore herself out? Apparently, his friend offered good money for me. The whole suggestion makes me feel sick. I can't wait to get away from him and his creepy friends."

He blows out a breath. "Okay, so what's the plan? You previously said the bar work is temporary."

"It is. I have an acceptance letter from a college in San Diego to study law. I want to specialize in family law. I start in the fall," I answer proudly.

"Wow, that's fantastic, congratulations!"

I blush at Cal's comment. It's the first genuine kind compliment I've received. The few women I've mentioned it to at the club have rolled their eyes or raised their eyebrows, my dad had blown his stack I was choosing to not work more hours and earn more money at the "whore house" instead. Apparently, I was wasting a good opportunity and good money.

"Sooo Cal, I've noticed you kind of avoid telling me about the business you work in, is there a reason for that?" I ask, running a finger over the brim of my coffee cup.

He pulls on his hair slightly as he runs his fingers through it. He looks away uneasily. "Yeah, the same reason I haven't told you my full name. I guess I just like it me and you and not all the crap that comes with my life."

Hmm, that was a loaded answer if ever there was one.

"Okay so by that I take it I'm not going to be impressed with the business you're in. This is Vegas, Cal. I've seen lots of strange, weird, dodgy things going on and I've also seen you. Nothing you tell me will stop how I feel toward you." I giggle.

He slumps back in his chair. Relieved? Dumbstruck?

A small smile curls on his face and he sits forward and grasps my hands in his. "Well, if I'm completely honest, I'm not always here for business. I kind of fell for a girl I met in a club and can't get her out of my head. So here I am, for you." He lays it all out on the line and it's my turn to be gobsmacked. It's also probably the sweetest thing anyone has ever said to me.

Although I know we have a connection and we flirt, I was waiting with bated breath for him to ask me out, anything really. I wasn't aware he was from the East Coast and made an effort that monumental just to come and see me.

"So, here's how I see it. I like you, you like me, I know your name's not Carmen and you know my business isn't legit, how about we just have today? Then tomorrow we lay it all out on the line?"

"You think I won't want you when I know what your business is?" I question.

"I intend to fight for you if that's the case, Carmen, but I also want to have just you, no disappointment, no expectations. Just me and you."

How the fuck do I refuse that? Easy, I don't.

I sit straighter, with purpose. "So, Cal, which hotel are you in?"

~

It had to be the biggest freaking suite at the most luxurious hotel, didn't it, to add to that small sliver of doubt and apprehension in my head.

Cal walks me backward into the suite, hands on my hips, peppering kisses down my neck, sucking gently on my collarbone. He nods to his left. "Bedroom," he pants as he slowly walks me into the direction of the bedroom.

My breath is rapid with trepidation, my legs feel shaky with nerves, and my pussy clenches with desperation. I've never felt so turned on and desperate.

I stop when my heel hits the bed. He's gasping for breath, his hard-on is flush up to his stomach. I lift my top as my chest heaves with anticipation. His gaze is scorching and the look in his eyes is fierce. My panties are wet and I squeeze my thighs together under his glare.

"Fuck, you're so goddamn hot, Carmen." He brushes his hair from his face, places his hands behind my neck, and pulls me in closer. He kisses me with so much passion I swear I'm ready to explode. His tongue sweeps my mouth and before I know it, I'm giving it back as good as I'm receiving it.

He unclasps my bra and it falls between us. His left hand moves to my breast and he explores, squeezing and brushing my nipple to a peak. I moan into his mouth.

"Fuck, Carmen, lose the pants. Fucking lose them," he says in a rush.

We both lose our pants at the same time. He tugs his top over his head with one hand. Like a fucking super model, his body is a sculptured temple, no fat in sight, lean with tight muscled shoulders and strong firm abs. He's wearing white boxers that show off his tanned skin, he has a V-line with a dark trail of hair. He raises his eyebrows and pushes his boxers down with a cocky smirk.

Holy fucking shit, his cock is fucking gorgeous. Is that possible? Cal has pre-cum sticking from the end to his stomach. It makes my mouth water and I lick my lips. His eyes dart to my lips as he fists his cock, tugging it three times as if to relieve some pressure.

He bends and slowly pulls my panties down my legs to my feet. I step out of them while remaining in eye contact with him, the heat palpable between us. With a gentle shove, he pushes me onto the bed.

Cal works his way up from my feet, slowly kissing me from the inside of my legs to the outside, gently sucking now and again, making my pussy clench. He knows what he's doing. I can feel the smile against my legs each time I moan.

"Jesus Cal, you're killing me here."

"What do you want, baby?"

"You. You, Cal, all of you."

He reaches my pussy and shoves his face into it, breathing in as if to embrace it. His tongue darts out and I almost shoot off the bed. He licks the crease of my groin on both sides and then painstakingly slowly works his way inward, sucking my folds into his mouth. Holy hell, that's hot.

Soft moans escape me. I'm struggling to remain in control and desperate to reach my orgasm, but I'm also enjoying his exploration. He sucks at my folds harder, as if to mark them, then he starts sucking at my clit. I arch my back off the bed, screaming, "Ah, ah, shit, Cal, just there, fuuucckkk."

Cal pushs his hands under my ass and lifts me to his face, encouraging me to push myself into him more. The roughness of the scruff on his chin makes my legs tingle. He twists his tongue inside me, back and forth, fucking me with his mouth. I completely lose control and scream his name, letting myself release. "Fuck, Callllllll."

I slowly come down from my orgasm. Wow, that was

incredible. I look down to Cal, whose eyes are twinkling mischievously, a smug grin on his face, he swipes his hand across his wet mouth and crawls up my body toward me. "You're so beautiful when you come," he grins.

I laugh as he gently grabs my face and kisses me. I can taste myself on his tongue and it only adds to my already eager state of arousal.

He rolls to the side of the bed and digs around for his wallet, retrieving a strip of condoms. He tears one off and with his teeth rips it open. He turns to me slowly and moves onto his knees. He looks me in the eyes as he rolls the condom on. My tongue darts out over my bottom lip and his eyes grow dark with arousal. He shuffles between my legs and we look at one another as he gently places a kiss on my lips and closes his eyes. "Beautiful." He pushes inside me and we both gasp gently in time with one another. Our eyes lock.

Cal stays still for a minute before he bites the inside of his mouth. "This is going to be over way too soon, Carmen, but I'll make it up to you, I promise," he says on a chuckle.

I lift my hand to his face, no words needed. He starts to move. He pistons in and out, in and out, rubbing me in all the right places. He slows his pace as he nips my breasts and tugs on my nipples, one at a time, suckling them into his mouth, slowly drawing me painfully closer to the pending edge. He expertly moves his hips from side to side, causing my clit to rub against his pubic bone. The man is a fucking sex god. My nails drill into his back as his thrusts become more erratic. Sweat coats his forehead. I've never seen a man so remarkably hot in my entire life.

"Fuck, Carmen, you're so fucking tight, baby. You're fucking perfect, so fucking soft and wet, I'm gonna lose my shit so fucking quick, baby got to go slow," he pants.

I can feel my orgasm building, I just need a little more. "No, move faster, Cal. I'm going to come soon."

He grabs my ass tightly in his palms, moving higher, shifting his hips, and driving into me with more force, quicker, tipping me over the edge.

"Ah, ffuuuuckkk, Cal."

"Fuck, baby!" he screeches.

I feel his cock swell and his breath stutter, his body jerk, and his movements slow. His head falls into the crook of my neck as he gasps for air. Our chests heave in unison. I stroke his sweaty hair from his forehead as he softly turns to face me. I kiss his forehead and smile. "That was amazing, Cal."

He smiles and kisses me passionately, his tongue sliding into my mouth.

"Yeah well, I could have lasted a bit longer but we've got all day and night," he says while wriggling his eyebrows, making me hit out at him with a playful grin.

Slowly Cal pulls off me and removes the condom, taking it to the bathroom. He returns and settles into bed next to me. I snuggle into his chest. We're both relaxed in a post-sex bubble.

I push farther up onto the pillow and gently stroke Cal's hair between my fingers. We are both high and contented.

Glancing down at the tattoo on his left shoulder, I ask, "What's with the wolf tattoo?"

"Family insignia. My da makes us all have one at sixteen. It's a sign of loyalty."

"Your da?" I giggle.

"Yeah, we're of Irish descent. You know, never been to Ireland, Da has never been to Ireland, but we're Irish, apparently," he says sarcastically as I laugh at him.

Cal's back straightens and his voice is low and soft, a little nervousness in it. "Irish Mafia to be precise." He stuns me with his confession and I stop brushing my hand through his hair. Cal sits higher so we're side by side, watching my face for a reaction.

"Do you deal in drugs, firearms, prostitutes? What, Cal?" I ask, trying to remain composed.

He blows out a worried breath. "Nothing involving humans, Carmen. More based on firearms and illegal clubs, gambling, fighting, that sort of thing, but nothing sexual or indecent." He looks at me from under his hair, awaiting a response.

I exhale. "Okay, I can deal with that." I nod, swallowing hard.

"You can?"

"Yeah, I mean it's not ideal but... I like you, Cal... really like you, actually, and I trust your judgment. I trust you."

He nods with a coy smile. "You should trust me, Carmen, I've never felt like this before, and..." He entwines his fingers with mine. "I don't know what this is between us right now but whatever it is, I don't want it to end. We're doing it, we're going to figure your school and shit out tomorrow, have a proper chat, and make a plan for the future, okay?"

"Yes," I reply with a small excited smile as he places his lips on mine.

"For now, we've other things to keep us busy..." he says, wriggling his eyebrows.

"Mmm, I couldn't agree with you more, Cal."

We spent the day being *busy* in bed. Cal brought me to orgasm multiple times, we had sex in the shower, gently in the bath, fast and desperate against the wall after dinner, and passionate again in bed into the night. I woke to an empty bed before the sun rose. Smelling the pillow beside me, I smile to myself.

I'm not naïve. I realize Cal has flaws being in the family business. I also realize that it was something he was pushed into and not something he was happy about doing. This didn't dissuade the soft affectionate Cal that he was. I knew he resented his father, and also he felt inadequate in his father's eyes. But I loved the Cal that was him, not the Cal his father wanted him to be. Jesus, did I love Cal? I smile at the thought.

Reluctantly, I move to the bathroom to relieve myself, washing my hands and looking in the mirror to see the marks Cal has left behind. I gently brush my fingers over the ones on my neck and look down at myself to find others dotted around my breast and stomach. I'm in a post-sex haze, smiling to myself, feeling like the luckiest woman alive —a woman who has been worshipped.

After a few minutes of reminiscing, I wonder if Cal is in the living area. He's being quiet if he is. "Cal, shall we order breakfast?" I call.

There's no answer and my stomach plummets. I pull the bathroom robe on and make my way into the living room. Cal's jacket and case are gone. I spin around to survey the area but nothing of Cal's remains. What the fuck? I move over to the dresser by the door and find a messy note and an envelope...

I'll be back, Cal

I open the envelope and I'm greeted with wads of cash. My body begins to shake. Who the hell leaves cash behind like this? What the hell is happening? I race back to the bedroom and grab my phone, but of course I don't have Cal's number, we haven't got that far. Why would he leave the cash and take his belongings?

Then it hits me. It fucking hits me like a freight train. He's used me, used me and then left a wad of money. Who does that? A payment? Jesus. I fall to the floor. I feel sick, I can't breathe and I feel dirty, used, and humiliated. He knows what my dad thinks of me, he knows how it hurts and now he's done this, left a fucking payment.

Fuck, how can I have been so stupid?

CHAPTER 8

Lily

I wake with a startle, noise and voices are coming from the kitchen. The clock reads 10:05. I freshen up in the bathroom, tug a hoodie on, and make my way toward the kitchen and living area. Cal is bent over the kitchen counter, deep in conversation with Bren and Oscar. As he looks directly at me, my heart stops. His eyes meet mine as he searches my face. I flick my gaze over his body, he looks so freaking hot!

I bite my lip to stop the thoughts going through my head. His gaze drops to my lip and he smirks. Bastard. I approach, I notice Cal's white leather couch is ripped.

No not ripped, destroyed—scratched and torn apart!

I dart my eyes to Cal for an explanation and spin on my feet, looking around. I can't see Reece so I assume he's still in his room. Cal tugs his hair. "Yeah, Pussy had a party with a laser pen last night." He points at the couch, shrugging.

"A party? Where the hell did he get a laser pen?"

"Apparently he lifted it from Oscar's keyring."

I look to Oscar. He shrugs and goes back to working on his tablet. They all seem completely unfazed by it. Me? I'd be fucking livid. I let out a sigh and decide to carry on. If they aren't bothered by it, then whatever.

"Don't worry, I confiscated the pen," Cal says as if to reassure me. "New couch will be delivered later." I roll my eyes at his nonchalance.

Fucking wow. These guys seem to have a bottomless pit of money. I shake my head in a huff. Whatever.

Oscar speaks up. He sounds nervous. "I hope you don't mind, Lily, but I've arranged for a doctor to come and assess Reece..." He puts his hands up in defense. "It's to help evaluate his medication and diagnoses."

I'm suddenly taken aback and blown away. I want to cry. I clear my throat. "Th...that's amazing, thank you!" I choke up.

All three men's shoulders relax instantly and they let out their breaths. Clearly, they were nervous making that call.

"Nico had a good doctor for us, but at the time, Reece was just diagnosed with ADHD so the medication was for that and then sleeping pills. But when things changed, you know when we left, I had him at various other doctors and a lot of them were contradicting each other and the medications were endless." I shake my head and exhale. It had all been such a minefield. One of my biggest struggles has been the guilt and desperation for Reece to receive the help, understanding, and support he deserves but it's always felt like a fight and completely out of reach, until now.

I look at the guys and hope they can hear my feelings through my words. "I'm really grateful for all your help and support, truly. You don't know how much this means to me, to us both." Cal nods at me with a reassuring smile, his loving blue eyes melt me.

Oscar straightens. Uncomfortable with the turn of conversation, he looks at me. "So next on the agenda, Reece's schooling..."

As if on cue, Reece strolls in with a serious case of bed head, his waves tangled into thick curls. "Mmm, I've chosen a school already. I just need Mom to sign off on it," he breezily tells us.

"Since when, Reece?" I ask, annoyed.

"I've been looking into it for a while. To be honest, it helped cement the decision to move here..." He waves his hand around the apartment.

Well, that shouldn't stun me, but it does. Cal brushes his hands through his hair, watching Reece as he helps himself to the orange juice.

"So, what happened at the old school?" Bren asks with a smug look. I glare at him, willing someone to beam me up and save me the embarrassment.

"Well...when we signed up at the school, this utter bitch secretary was looking down her nose at Mom and asked her twice"—Reece holds two fingers up to emphasize his point —"if she could afford the fees, fucking nosy cow. If you'd seen how she looked at Mom you'd have done the same as me," he says, nodding heavily to the three men.

"So what did you do?" Bren asks with a smile. This time it's Cal glaring at him as Oscar stands transfixed with arms folded at his front, listening intuitively.

"I did a little digging, that's what I did. And that digging taught me that Mrs. Nosy Bitch was fucking the married principal! On his desk! In a school uniform! So I filmed it. Then when it was assembly, I played it on the big screen in front of the entire school and PTA. Oh, and sent a copy of the files to both their partners so they'd know what cheating fuckers they're married to."

I shake my head, reliving the drama.

The guys look at one another in awe. Cal chokes on a laugh and then Bren really laughs. Oscar rubs his chin, eyebrows joined together. "How'd they know it was you?"

"Easy, I told them. I wanted them to know it was me, I wanted them to know you don't fuck with my mom or upset her, or ask her if she can afford things. Cheeky bitch."

"So you did that knowing you'd get thrown out?" Bren asks in confusion.

"Yeah," Reece replies, then shrugs and walks over to the TV, done with the conversation. I shrug at the three guys.

As I walk up to the guys, Cal turns to me and softly says, "I put your breakfast in the oven. We're heading out to sort things with Da. The results came back positive this morning."

I glance at him with a nod. He leans down, gently grabbing my head and peppers kisses against my forehead. "Thank you for giving me a son, Lily." My heart squeezes and I choke up. I lower my head, move away from him, and nod to disguise my tears.

"Sam's outside the door, phone on the counter is yours with our contact information, should you need it."

I can only reply through tears, "Thank you."

"See you later," the three of them shout in unison.

CAL

We're a few minutes into the drive to our family estate when my mind wanders back to Oscar arriving this morning. I'd been plagued during the night about Lily and Reece keeping something from me last night. I knew they were close and there was more to their past, but I didn't like being excluded from it. To move forward as a family we needed to be honest and united.

I'd asked Oscar to review the surveillance in the apartment. He called me into the den to show me the moment Reece had called Lily. Oscar zoomed in and increased the volume.

"Can you remember what I told you at Nico's about the rooms having eyes?" Reece asks. Lily nods her head in response.

"They have them here too. Just be aware, okay?"

She nods again while glancing up at the camera pointing at them, then just as quickly looks away.

"We need to let Greg know we're safe."

My stomach plummets at this point.

"I know. Leave it with me," Lily replies.

As she walks away, her eyes dart around the room, scanning for cameras.

Oscar spoke gently, breaking the silence and dread in my stomach. "They have a lot of secrets, Cal."

I nod my head, anxiety racing through me. "Yeah, I know, Oscar. They need to fucking tell us so we can help them. This secret whispering bullshit puts me on edge. They're capable of disappearing, what if they go again?" I drag my hand through my hair in desperation. I can't lose them. Not when I've only just found them.

"They won't. Reece came to us for protection. The kid's a fucking genius, he knew he was out of his depth. They won't go anywhere," he reassures me, piercing my eyes with his, willing me to believe him.

"What about this Greg guy?"

Oscar rubs his chin. "I don't know. We don't know anything about him other than he's on a pedestal for supposedly saving them."

"Put extra security on the door. I don't want them going anywhere without us knowing. Also, get some sort of tracking device on them."

Oscar nods in agreement.

Bren speaks and brings me out of my thoughts. "Da's gonna pitch a fit when he hears this shit today. Don't expect him to throw a happy family reunion party."

"I'm not fucking naïve, Bren." I snap, my patience thin this morning with the building tension surrounding the family fucking meeting.

"I've been thinking don't tell him about the cartel either," Bren adds.

"Agreed."

Oscar speaks up. "Don't mention Reece's capabilities. He'd use the kid and not in a good way. We need to teach

Reece there's a time and place to use his abilities and not let assholes exploit him."

I'm momentarily stunned at my little brother's suggestion. He's being protective over Reece, and this is not the first time. Oscar never shows much emotion and never gave us any indication he was capable of caring for someone.

He isn't like me and Connor, who wear our hearts on our sleeves. He isn't like Bren and Finn who are the epitome of heartless. No, Oscar is usually empty and void of any emotion, so to hear him acting protective and caring is a shock. Bren looks at me in the rearview mirror, obviously thinking the same.

CHAPTER 9

Cal

We arrive at the estate and go through the usual security protocols at the gate, then drive around the back. Ma comes out of the kitchen door and greets us with a smile on her face. Her smiles have never been the same since Keenan died. When she smiles, it doesn't reach her eyes.

We get out of the car. "Your da's inside, Con and Finn are there already. Will I be joining you or is this a business meeting?" she asks delicately.

I kiss Ma's cheek. "You'll be joining us." She follows us inside.

We sit at the family table, Da at the top, Bren and I sit either side, Oscar sits beside me, Finn and Con opposite, with Ma on the end opposite Da.

"Well, I hope this is going to be good. I struggled to get out of bed this morning." Con sighs with a lazy yawn, his wavy hair wild and unruly.

"I struggled to get out of a blonde!" Finn counters, snickering to himself.

Da speaks next. "What's this fuckin' 'bout, Cal? Spit it feckin' out. You look like shit, what the fuck ya done?"

I clear my throat and rub my hair. "Well, recently it came to my attention that I have a son." I let out quickly.

Gasps are released around the table, my knee bouncing with nerves. "And?" Da snaps.

I clear my throat. "And he's mine, the DNA test has confirmed it. I'm claiming him as mine, his birth certificate will be changed accordingly."

"How old is he?" Finn asks gently.

"Fourteen," I quickly respond.

Da blows up. Here we fucking go... "Fourteen. Fourteen? Ya have a kid that's feckin' fourteen and you only just found out? Or did the bitch keep him from ya?"

Oscar bristles at Da's derogatory words toward Lily. Again Oscar has impressed me.

"No, she didn't keep him from me. We didn't know each other's full personal details back then and like I said, we've recently reconnected and I learned about Reece," I reply in a firm voice, feeling pissed I was even having to explain myself to him, the dick.

"Well, tell her you'll have the kid, pay her off or somethin', and then fuck her off. We don't need any more shit in our lives, we've got too much going on 'ere!" He waves his hand around.

I straighten my back. What a fucking prick. Fuck her off? Pay her off? As if you fucking suggest that to anyone.

"Well, that's not happening," I respond, snapping back at him, my eyes drilling him.

All the guys sit straighter in their chairs, prepared for a fight. Bren's eyebrow is raised, Finn's sitting with a grin and chewing a fucking toothpick. Cocky little shit, he's enjoying the show.

"You walk into my house to tell me you have a bastard son, expect me to accept him at fourteen, then try telling me what's going to happen?" He blows the words out, attempting to stay controlled.

"Yeah, Da, that's exactly what I'm doing. And he won't be a bastard son when I marry his mother, and if you want to accept him you can, if not then..." I shrug.

I'm past giving a crap what this asshole thinks. He doesn't get to disrespect Reece or Lily and I won't bring them here until he realizes that.

He shoots out of his chair, launches at my face, and smacks me straight in the jaw, the fucking prick. Fuck, that hurt. I rub the spot.

His chair falls backward and he thumps both fists on the table, making the table and us all jump in unison.

His face is thunderous and he spits the words out. "You ain't feckin' marrying her so get that right out your fucking dumb head, ya useless piece of shit. Ya marrying that Saunders girl like I arranged." He stabs his finger into his chest. "I arranged, not you, me. Because we know you can't fucking arrange a damn thing. Fuckin' useless, couldn't even produce an heir inside of feckin' wedlock, you stupid little cunt. Now ya think you're risking all I've done for a piece of fucking pussy? Over my dead fucking body, lad!"

I swipe the blood from my lip and breathe out. "Well I'm sorry to disappoint but one way or another I'll find a way out of this marriage and when I have, I'll be marrying Lily. But don't worry, Da, I'll make sure it doesn't upset your business plans," I retort sarcastically. My chest is heaving in frustration. There's no fucking way he's keeping me from pursuing my family.

Ma jumps up and pours Da a whiskey, which he drinks in one go and then clicks his fingers for another. Condescending prick.

"So, who's the girl?" Connor asks with a knowing smile.

"Lily, the girl I met in Vegas." I smile back.

Finn whistles under his breath.

Con nods with an approving smile in my direction and Ma looks at me and beams a smile. It lights up her face. She's happy for me.

They all know about Lily, the girl that got away in Vegas. They all put up with me wallowing in self-pity for months after she left. Da took it upon himself to hire me numerous escorts to "help me get over the pussy." He's a heartless prick and it wasn't the first time I'd wondered if he was capable of love or compassion.

"When do we get to meet them?" Ma asks.

"Whenever Da has calmed the fuck down." I scrub my hand through my hair, scowling in his direction. This makes all the guys look at me. They know it's a nervous trait of mine. Bren nods in encouragement. "I need to get a few things straight about Reece first. He's a little different than normal kids his age."

Finn stops chewing his toothpick, eyes narrowed in confusion. Oscar shuffles uncomfortably.

"Different how?" Con asks.

"He's on the autistic spectrum. He doesn't like touching, he says what he thinks without actually thinking, he likes his technology." I try to keep it brief, but so they'll be aware when meeting him.

Finn looks at me and speaks with a smug smile. "Can't wait to meet the little cherub." He grins.

I flip him the bird, causing the cocky shit to chuckle.

Da, who's now retrieved his chair and is sitting back on

it, throws his head back, shoulders straight, palms slapping on the table. "Fan-feckin-tastic. Another feckin' weirdo in the family."

This is aimed at Oscar, who apart from straightening slightly, continues typing on his tablet, ignoring the arrogant bastard's comments.

"Oi, enough, Da. It's a good fucking job Oscar is a weirdo, otherwise your shit out-of-date security methods would have put us all in jeopardy countless times and your sorry ass would have been in the ground long ago, so leave him the fuck alone," Bren bellows.

Everyone falls silent, including Da.

Da clucks his tongue in thought. "Didn't say I didn't approve of him, just said I don't know if we have room in the family for another weirdo." He shrugs as if he's not saying anything wrong.

"Well on that note, Da, I'm off. Let me know when you've decided if you've room in the family for *both* Reece and Lily," I say with an exaggerated smile.

I slap Oscar on the back and he jumps to his feet. All three on the other side follow. I give Ma a kiss and she squeezes my arm in support.

As we leave the kitchen into the fresh fucking air, Finn and Con congratulate me with pats on the back and laughing about Da's face and the fact he hadn't died on the spot. This makes Oscar smirk. We make our way to the car, Bren's driving, but before he opens the door he turns to me. "Proud of you bro, proud you stuck up for both of them too."

This means a lot from Bren, who never says anything remotely supportive or caring to anyone.

CHAPTER 10

Lily

I pace the living room, biting my nails. I'm so nervous for Cal to visit his family. I know they'll have a problem with our current situation. I'm also nervous about the text I've just sent with one of the burner phones. I feel I'm betraying Cal by hiding them but at the same time, I owe Greg my loyalty. I owe him my life and my son's life. Still, I feel the nagging sense of betrayal in the pit of my stomach.

I busy myself around the apartment, making the beds in all the rooms. I clean the kitchen, anything to take my mind off the dread in my stomach. I make my way to the laundry room and just as I start folding the washing, I feel the hairs on the back of my neck rise. My breathing escalates when I smell his presence. Before I can turn around, he's pushed his chest into my back and his hand is caressing my stomach lovingly.

"I can't tell you how much I love coming home to you being here, Lily." His voice is gravelly and I can feel his hard-on pressed into my ass. The heat is rising from my chest into my face. I squeeze my legs together. God, he affects me so much, right down to my core.

Cal takes the panties I'm folding from my hands and runs his fingers through them, rubbing them.

"I can't tell you how much I love having your panties in my hand as well." He moves his mouth to my ear. "I prefer them wet, when you take them off..."

I spin around to face him, his hands dart to my hips to hold me there. As I look up to his lust-filled eyes, my eyes narrow in on his lip—his busted lip.

"What the hell happened to your lip, Cal?" Yep, I killed the moment.

"Da was a little pissed. It went better than expected though, so that's good." He laughs.

He moves his hand down my face. "You're so fucking beautiful, baby. God, I've missed you so fucking much." His lips linger over mine and slowly they move in. The kiss is soft, gentle, and loving. He coaxes my mouth open.

Cal's hands tighten on my hips, my breath hitching, my hands moving to cup his face. I open my mouth wider and he explores it with his tongue, deeper and more sensual. I moan into his mouth as he pushes himself harder onto me.

"Fuck, baby, you've no idea what you do to me," he says as he rubs his groin against my stomach.

He starts lifting my T-shirt at the side when a screeching high-pitched alarm vibrates through the apartment. We disconnect in an instant, Cal withdrawing a weapon from behind his back. He screams at me to stay put and is gone in a flash.

I freeze for only seconds, then I realize I need to get to Reece. I don't think twice, running down the corridor toward the kitchen as smoke plumes through the apartment. Shit.

"What the fuck, Reece?" I hear Cal shout.

I approach the kitchen and visibly relax when I see a worried-looking Reece and an exploded microwave.

Cal's stare is enough to strike you dead on the spot. Security is already there and has stopped the alarm.

"What's happened? What have you done, Reece?" I'm breathing heavily, panic evident in my voice.

"Our son has tried to make a fucking bomb!"

My eyes come out of my head, I swear to god! I gasp. "A fucking bomb? What the hell, Reece? Jesus, you could have killed us, Reece. I'm so fucking pissed with you right now. Do you have any idea how dangerous that is? Do you even care? Get the fuck out of my sight this instant." I'm screaming so loud my head pounds, tears escape my eyes, and I'm shaking.

"I was just trying to do a bit of chemistry homework," he grumbles while leaving the room.

I look at Cal as a silent sorry. He looks at me and his face softens. He walks toward me and tucks hair behind my ear and gently holds my face. "It's okay, baby. I'll sort it, don't worry."

What have I done to deserve him? He's taken all this in stride and one look from me and he melts, making me melt, and I instantly know everything is going to be okay.

I shake my head. "It's not okay, Cal. I'm so sorry we've come into your life and completely turned it upside down. I'm sorry we're ruining all this." I fling my arms up and down the apartment.

"Shhh, baby, don't say that. Fuck, I need you guys as much as you need me. I've told you, a part of me was missing until I had you and I never want to feel like that again. You're both where you belong, you hear me?"

I nod, even though I can't understand how he can feel that way with the trouble we're causing.

"You go shower. I'll sort this." I nod again robotically in response.

CAL

I get the staff to tidy the kitchen and hire a painter to come tomorrow to sort the wall damage.

I spoke to Oscar, who's agreed to assess the Internet firewall to ensure Reece has stronger Internet restrictions in place. Hopefully, the little shit won't be turning into a terrorist anytime soon.

We also agreed the sooner he is in school, the better. He needs somewhere to engage his ever-inquisitive mind.

The school Reece suggested is actually at the top of Oscar's list too. Its security is high-end, it has a gifted and talented wing, its multicultural and bilingual, and bodyguards are allowed into the classroom.

I order Thai for dinner. When Lily comes back from her shower, she's a little down but seems more relaxed as the evening goes on.

I don't know how she's managed fourteen years with Reece on her own, let alone struggling with money and being a new mother. She'd gained my utmost respect in every aspect. I have no doubt she's an amazing mother. She was fucking perfect.

We lay on the couch together, her between my legs. I stroke her hair and massage her head as Reece sits on the other end with Puss. It didn't escape me that Reece was also stroking and massaging the cat. It makes me smile to myself. It also made me realize if I could have a perfect night, other than Lily being on her back with me between her legs, this would be it.

We've chatted intermittently. She's told me about her background in law and how she hopes to continue that in the future. I'd explained to Lily that I was going to be working in the warehouse office a lot this coming week as we had shipments due in. After the previous month's shipments had been fucked up, by no other than our friends the Russians—in particular Igor Dimitriev—we were making sure we covered all angles this week.

CHAPTER 11

Lily

I t had turned into a busy week with Cal working long hours and sometimes coming in late at night. I'd leave him a meal in the oven with a note. I knew he came into my room and checked on me before going to bed, I could sense him there.

Reece had seen a doctor and his medication had been adjusted. I was so grateful for the support the family was giving me. We got Reece signed up to a new school.

Sam, our appointed bodyguard, had taken us to the mall for new clothes and gaming items for Reece. He also chose new paints and furniture for his room, making it more personal and comfortable for him. All in all, we were settling in well.

It's now Friday and I'm straightening Reece's shirt. He's fidgeting and fussing about the collar being buttoned but I want him to look smart for Cal, who is taking him to meet his fiancée.

The thought of them together, all three of them, made

me feel sick, but his father had insisted on him doing this before accepting Reece into the family. Cal said it was a control thing and he was trying to manipulate them because Cal had "put his foot down and overruled" him during the family meeting.

Reece pulls on his shiny rain jacket with the hood and proceeds to pull his hood up over his neatly combed hair. I sigh and turn to see Cal approach with a questionable smile, his lip turned up at the side.

He looks and smells gorgeous and that just makes me feel worse. I deflate internally with a loud sigh.

Cal immediately senses I'm uncomfortable. "Lily, listen. This is a one-off thing. I've no intention of making this something regular and I've no intention of Penelope having any relationship with Reece. In fact, I've no intention of her being around Reece at all," he says with sincerity.

"I know, Cal, you keep saying that but here we are..." I lift my arm up and down to emphasize the fact that both he and Reece are dressed up to meet another woman, his fiancée.

"Please behave, Reece, I don't want Penelope to think I haven't raised you well." Cal frowns at me, leans in, and kisses me on my cheek. I'm sure it's to reassure me but it doesn't.

CAL

Reece and I arrive at La Violla restaurant at 12:55 p.m. We're meeting Penelope here at 1:00 p.m. Of course the bitch couldn't arrive on time. Nope, thirty-five minutes later and we're still waiting like idiots. My frustrations are growing and my patience wearing thin.

"I'm hungry and thirsty and Mom said you were going to feed me and where the fuck is your fiancée? I'm fucking starving and fucking thirsty and I'm not fucking happy. Why the fuck couldn't we go somewhere that lets you bring cats? What the fuck is wrong with people, not liking fucking cats anyway?" Reece rants.

I sigh and exhale, frustrated and annoyed for myself but also frustrated and annoyed for Reece. She's setting herself up to fail in his eyes, but she doesn't fucking care. This is typical fucking Penelope Saunders.

Finally, the doors swing open and in walks the plastic bimbo herself, my fucking fiancée. Dread fills my stomach.

"Ooo, Cal," she screeches in that annoying as fuck whiney voice, waving her bony elongated fingers in my direction. I cringe when I glance around and see eyes on us. How the fuck can my dad think this is acceptable?

She's teetering on the highest heels, with the skimpiest white dress known to man, no bra, showing her big plastic nipples to the whole fucking restaurant. I want to curl up in a ball and fucking die, my eyes are burning from the fucking embarrassment and my balls shrivel to peanuts at the mere thought of touching her.

I glance at Reece while exhaling and gathering a little courage to welcome her. His eyes are bulging out of his head and I'm quickly aware that my son is a teenager and she may well be a walking, talking wet dream to him. Shit, fuck, Jesus, I cannot cope! My hand brushes through my hair in frustration as I gasp at the realization.

My concerns quickly dissipate when Reece's reaction dawns on me. His facial expressions cannot be concealed, and his face? Yeah, pure and utter repulsion. That's my boy. His glare is venomous and sheer disgust oozes from him.

"OMG, why would you let him wear that jacket in here?" she snipes, her eyes transfixed on Reece. Not even a hello.

I turn to face Penelope slowly. Please tell me she did not try to insult my son.

"Penelope, it's a fucking rain jacket, get a fucking grip and your head out your stuck-up ass, nobody cares what he wears. He's a fucking kid!"

"Erm, exccc...cuse me." she drags the word out. "I care, because I have a social standing and Insta reputation to uphold, and if he wants to be seen out with me, and you, you'd both better start wearing what is expected of you. You won't be dragging me down the gutter with you both." She glares at Reece before surveying him from top to bottom as though he's a piece of shit. Her lips open in disgust as her eyes sneer in his direction. My fists clench.

Reece is thankfully oblivious because he's now wandering around the waiting area, cautiously poking his head around doors, lifting ornaments with interest, and looking at plants a little too hard. Yeah, the kid is bored as fuck.

"Let's just go and sit, shall we?" I suggest through tightened lips.

We need to hurry up and get the hell out of here before I say something more. She huffs and trots along in front of us to the reserved circular table. Clearly she's had ass implants too, she can barely fucking walk, it's more of a shuffle and those ass cheeks don't look even.

Reece follows me, looking bewildered, completely out of his comfort zone and I feel for him. It's an upmarket restaurant and it's not somewhere I'd have chosen to bring a child, that's for sure.

We arrive at our table and Penelope is standing behind her chair. I look at her and raise my eyebrow in question.

"I'm waiting for you to pull out my chair, Cal," she proudly announces, flicking her long fake platinum hair behind her.

Yeah, good luck with that. Bitch. Not after insulting my son. I huff and ignore her, taking my place next to her. Reece follows next to me.

She's still standing there as I open a menu for Reece. The next thing I know, she's clicking her fingers above her head, her head darting around like an alert meerkat.

Reece looks at me. "Cal, what's she doing?" he whispers.

"Not got a clue, buddy." I look around, grimacing at the scene she's making, and want to crawl under the fucking table. I hide behind the menu.

"Assistance, assistance," she screeches. Good god, someone shoot her. That's not a bad idea—if worse comes to worst that's something Oscar can look into. My mind begins to wander.

Bringing me out of my daze, a server arrives and asks her if he can help. "Yes, I need you to pull out my chair." She cannot be fucking serious. I glare at her and this time it's her huffing as she settles down in her seat, shuffling her uneven ass from side to side.

"Cal, I thought it was rude to click your fingers at people?" Reece asks quietly.

"It is, dude." Jesus, my fourteen-year-old autistic son has more manners.

She clicks her fingers again and Reece's eyes pop out of his head, followed by his eyebrows furrowing with a sharp intense stare. He looks like a fucking serial killer right now. I brush my hand through my hair, I need a fucking drink ASAP.

The server arrives and she wants her fucking napkin placed on her knee. He tells me he'll be back shortly to take our drinks and food order, thank fuck for that.

We sit in silence as Penelope proceeds to take selfies at every possible angle. Reece is watching her with a revolted curiosity on his face. He tilts his head from side to side, blatantly scrutinizing her.

"What's wrong with her lips?" he asks.

I choke on my water. "She's had lip fillers to make them bigger," I try to explain with my mouth twitching into a smirk at his confused expression.

"Why?"

"I don't know, buddy, it's something women do some-times." I shrug, unsure how to explain the mind of a nutjob like her.

"Well, what's up with her nose then?"

"I think she had surgery on her nose because she didn't like it," I reply.

He's tipping his head from side to side again as if trying to analyze her.

"Well, she looks fucking ugly, Cal, and plastic-looking too!" he says with all seriousness.

I can't help but stifle a laugh at that. I'm just about to lecture him in not letting Penelope hear him when my phone buzzes. Shit, it's Bren, I need to take this call.

"Penelope, can you keep an eye on Reece, please? I really need to take this call. Order me a steak and a scotch and whatever Reece wants to eat and drink please," I tell her. She huffs in protest, but I pay no attention as I quickly exit the restaurant into the waiting area.

Bren proceeds to tell me that he's set up surveillance in Igor Dimitriev's office while having a meeting there earlier today. We're due a shipment this evening, so we're hoping to pick up some intel from their office that may lead us to discover what's been happening with our missing deliveries. We agree to meet back at my apartment this evening to listen in.

Before I know it, I've been speaking to him for twenty minutes, so I cut the call and head back to the table.

Reece is engrossed in his tablet and Penelope is tapping away on her phone. I sit down and drink the scotch in one to give me some much-needed relief.

"So, Penelope, what's new," I ask her, not caring for a reply while I'm tearing into the bread roll.

"Oh, I brought the most amazing dress for the pre-bach-elorette party, it's to die for!"

My stomach sinks, I roll my eyes and grunt in response.

"Will Reece be wanting to attend the wedding? I don't mean to sound mean, Cal, but I didn't know about him when the invites went out, and I'm not sure he exactly fits in with the type of wedding me and Daddy have in mind," she says, waving her hands toward Reece.

I look from her to him. Is she for fucking real? How fucking heartless can this bitch be?

"My son is sitting right here, Penelope, do not speak about him as though he isn't. He will not *want* to come to the wedding, I'm surprised any fucker would *want* to come to any wedding you attend let alone hold yourself..." I'm getting louder, seething, but fortunately, I'm abruptly cut off when the server arrives with our meals, it's probably a good thing. I breathe deeply to calm my anger. The fucking nerve of her.

I offer the server a tight thank you with a strained smile.

I look to Reece after a few moments. He's pulling his hair, visibly upset with something. He's rocking slightly and I realize he's probably heard all our conversation and that's probably why he's so upset. He rocks backward and forward in the chair, an anguished noise coming from him. Shit, what the fuck do I do? Panic envelops me.

The next thing I know, he proceeds to tip his plate up, throwing it over the table in absolute horror.

I look from him to the meal to try and figure out what the hell is happening.

"I can't fucking eat that, it's got green shit on it, Cal, fucking on it, on the burger, and the cheese, Cal, it's orange," he spits. Then he grabs for the salad and throws the sliced tomato toward Penelope. "Red doesn't touch fucking green!" he announces, his hands shaking.

Reality dawns on me. Yeah, I fucked up and left him to his own devices. Shit, I'm a crap dad. I quickly divert my eyes to his drink. Coke! Fucking hell, he's ordered Coke. I quickly shift it out of his reach while the servers gather to help tidy up.

Penelope's whines and protests can be heard above the other chaos, as though she's the one needing the most assistance at the minute, for a fucking tomato on her dress.

Reece is beside himself, rocking and tugging on his hair, mumbling to himself. I help the servers and apologize profusely. They assure me everything is fine and nod toward Reece with understanding in their eyes. They show more compassion than the woman beside me who is so wrapped up in herself she hasn't even asked what or why this occurred, she's so fucking self-absorbed.

My heart is pounding against my chest with anxiety. I don't know how the fuck Lily has dealt with this.

Eventually, I coax Reece to settle down when I explain he can order dessert, which he promptly accepts with a portion of fries.

One ice cream is delivered in next to no time.

I sit back in my chair with a deep exhale, crisis a-fucking-verted, thank fuck.

Reece is sitting with his tablet, chuckling to himself, eating his fries, dipping them in his ice cream, when Penelope announces, "I cannot wait for you to see Toodles and Poodles on our wedding day, Cal. They have the cutest little outfits and their fur is going to be dyed bright pink," her eyes popping with excitement.

I'm in a bit of a daze listening to her but she has grabbed Reece's attention. "Who are Toodles and Poodles?" he asks innocently.

She claps her hands together loudly like a moron, bringing attention to us from other tables. "They're my babies, they're little Pomeranians," she replies with her whiny bimbo voice.

"They're dogs? You're going to dye your dogs' fur?" Reece asks with an annoyed tone to his voice. Oh shit.

"Yes, absolutely. They've grown to love being pampered, just like their mommy!" She smiles through bulging lips.

"Are you going to give them lip fillers too? Do you realize how inhumane you're being, treating those poor animals as dress-up dolls?" He sneers.

Yeah, I'm gonna let him ride this conversation out. I sit back and watch with an internal smile.

Penelope shifts on her chair, her tone turning rotten. "My dogs are my business. Nobody is asking you to look at them and you won't be coming to *my* wedding so don't worry about it."

Wow, she even argues like a fucking child. I smile to myself and give Reece a nonchalant look, a do-your-worst look.

"Well, I've a good mind to call animal welfare on you. Part of me wishes they'd bite your ratty nose off, but I wouldn't want them to be infected with the poison inside you and I don't mean all the fillers and Botox you've had."

I smirk to myself. Ha, my boy is good. I sit and watch them both, my head flicking between them.

Penelope taps her ridiculously long fingernails on the table, then glares at Reece. Raising an eyebrow while smirking, she clicks her fingers high in the air, knowing full well Reece is less than impressed with her spoiled condescending manners.

Reece looks at me quickly, then smirks to himself before putting his head down and concentrating on his tablet. I look at him a little shocked and confused. I didn't think he'd give up on the conversation that easily but if I'm honest, I'm relieved. I've had enough and as soon as Penelope has eaten the dessert she's ordered through the poor haggard server, we'll be leaving.

Penelope sits straighter, shuffling her smug ass on the chair, clearly feeling triumphant and pleased with herself for annoying Reece and me. She's smiling to herself, at least I think that's what she's trying to do, but her lips barely move with all the fucking filler she has in them.

Reece begins shuffling around and puts his tablet on the floor under the table. He slips his rain jacket on, tipping his hood up with a smirk on his lips. I look at him in confusion, just as an alarm sounds and the restaurant sprinkler system kicks in.

What I can only describe as all-out complete and utter fucking panic ensues, water spurts out of the sprinklers. It's fucking freezing!

Guests start screaming and covering themselves with jackets or they crawl under the tables. Servers are frantic, management staff run around, trying to figure out what the hell is happening.

Penelope is screeching. I turn to her and she looks like a drowned fucking rat with her thick mascara running down her face, her hair clinging to her, her fake as fuck nipples exposed. Her blubbering fat lips make her look almost comical.

The whole restaurant is soaked, apart from my son in his fucking rain jacket with his hood up and a smile on his face. I don't know whether to wring the little shit's neck or laugh at the spectacular fucking prank.

CHAPTER 12

Cal

We arrive back at the apartment drenched. Lily greets us at the door.

"Erm, are you wet, Cal?" she asks cautiously, her eyes darting to the window in search of the illusive rain.

She's beautiful and I love her, but is she for fucking real right now?

"Yes, Lily, I'm fucking drenched, but don't worry, Reece here is pretty dry in comparison. Right, Buddy?" I snap.

Lily's face drops when the realization hits her that Reece is at fault in some way. Reece shrugs off my veiled accusation and skulks off to his room.

"Cal, are you ok? What happened?" she asks, her voice laced with panic.

I brush my hand through my hair. I'm at the zero-patience point at this minute and the look on my face must have insinuated just that.

"I'll go and make you a coffee. Why don't you go and

shower? Bren and Oscar are in the den," she calls, walking toward the kitchen.

I shower in record time and pull on loose sweats and a T-shirt. I enter the kitchen and walk to Lily, who has her back to me. I bracket my hands around her waist, pushing my chest to her back, and gently kiss her neck, lingering my lips just under her ear. "I'm sorry I snapped at you."

She slowly turns around. "It's okay, Cal. Believe me, I know how difficult Reece can be, and in public too? I get it, please don't apologize. You're doing amazing." Fuck, I needed that reassurance.

Lily stretches onto her tiptoes and kisses my lips gently. This is the first time she's initiated a kiss and I close my eyes and linger my lips on hers longer. I move my hands down from her hip to her ass and squeeze. She lets out a small moan and her hands go behind my head to my neck, gently caressing my hair. She pushes herself into me. My tongue slips through her mouth and the kiss becomes frantic.

I'm rock hard and push myself into her farther, grinding into her stomach to give myself some relief. Fuck, that feels good.

A throat clears loudly, making us pull apart. "Fuck, Bren, seriously?" I snarl.

My brother chuckles, rolling back on his heels. "Hate to fucking cockblock you love birds, but we really need to listen in on this conversation." I nod my head, kiss Lily's nose, and reluctantly slip away.

I walk into the den. "You sure know how to pick your fucking moments, dipshit. My cock has never been so fucking hard," I grumble to both my brothers.

"Yeah, we can fucking see." Bren snickers and glares at my pants.

I roll my eyes. "Whatever, this best be good!" I pull my hand down my face in frustration.

Oscar turns the volume up and we listen in to the scene playing out on the screen. Igor, the leader of the Russian gang that we suspect of stealing our goods, is sitting back in his chair like the arrogant kingpin that he was. His face is badly scarred from a severe burn he received as a teenager. "We had Bren here today. They suspect something, I'm sure of it," he explains to Symon, his younger brother.

They began to speak Russian and we all look to one another, pissed that we can't understand what they're saying.

Banging on the door interrupts our thoughts, startling Oscar.

"Hey, let me in fuckers," Reece calls.

I sigh dramatically and pinch the bridge of my nose. I've seriously had my fill of him today.

Bren chuckles to himself. "Sucks to be you right now, hey Cal?"

Oscar glares at him, stands up, and opens the door to Reece.

Before the door is fully open, Reece barges in and is spinning around the room in awe. We all watch him with curiosity.

"So, what are you guys having a meeting about?"

"Nothing, Reece," I snap. He glares at me for being sharp.

Oscar speaks first. "We bugged an office earlier and we were just listening in on the conversation before they started talking in their mother tongue. Now we don't know what they're saying."

I look to Bren, raising my eyebrows. I'm taken aback that Oscar, who is usually so closely guarded with intel, is explaining this situation to my fourteen-year-old son. Bren looks at me, clearly pissed too, his jaw ticking.

Reece glances toward the monitor. "Mmm, the Dimitriev brothers. Wankers," he asserts.

How the fuck does he know them? I straighten in my chair.

Bren scoffs and throws himself back in the chair. My eyes bug out and Oscar has an amused expression on his face that makes me question his motives.

"Let me guess, you dumb fucks don't speak Russian? Even my mom speaks some fucking Russian. Greg insisted on it. Okay, go on then, rewind the tape," Reece declares, rolling his eyes at us while motioning with his hand for Oscar to rewind the tape.

Oscar does as he instructs, and we watch from the background as Reece listens attentively to the conversation. He stops the tape partway through to inform us of the conversation. "Symon said to start talking in Russian when discussing the Irish job, it wasn't safe to talk about it in English. Igor said the shipment will arrive on time at 2:00 a.m., but the cargo ship was sent early to avoid detection of the ship awaiting. Symon asked if the transfer ship was going back to Port Newark like before."

I look at my son astounded. He's walked in here and in minutes solved so many questions we'd been striving to resolve.

"So basically, they know when our cargo ships leave, paying someone off to get them to depart earlier? Intercepting the cargo while at sea, the ship arrives seemingly untouched and on time with cargo missing. Therefore, nothing is happening at the warehouse," Bren states.

"Exactly! Now who do we fuck up first?" I clip back with excitement.

Bren taps his finger to his chin in thought. "I'm sending Finn and his team to the shipment loading yard. He can resolve that one. Con can wait at the warehouse and greet the captain and crew of the ship, see if they're innocent." Bren smiles with murderous glee in his eyes.

"Me and you Cal. We'll pay our little Russian friends a visit tomorrow." I nod to him, pleased as fuck this is finally coming together.

Reece sits with his arms folded, looking like the king of the castle. Smug shit. "I'll keep an eye on that little shit Boris on Monday." He nods to himself.

I look at Reece in question, "Boris?"

"Yeah, Boris Dimitriev, Symon's fucking spawn." Reece's tone is venomous.

"Where will you see Boris?" What the fuck is he talking about now? I swear to god my head is fucking spinning!

"At fucking school. Why do you think I chose that school? Fucking hell, Cal, I researched where that little shit went and decided to keep a close eye on him." He taps the side of his head in confirmation.

I drop my head in my hands and start breathing heavier, tugging my hair. This cannot be fucking happening! He's going to start an all-out fucking war, if not Monday then some fucking day. I snap my eyes up to Bren who's chuckling to himself, always such the smug fucking comedian, I hope he has a fucking girl and I hope to fuck she's a fucking promiscuous little shit, that'd teach him.

Oscar clears his throat, easing the tension. "Well Reece, I must say I'm very impressed. Now I have a little something here for you as a thank you."

Reece's demeanor changes and his face is alight with curiosity. In that moment, he makes me acutely aware that underneath all his knowledge, he's still just a kid, because let's face it— what kid doesn't like gifts? He suddenly appears so childlike, it makes my heart clench with the realization I never knew my son as a child. Fuck, that hurts. I rub at my chest in an attempt to disperse the pain.

Oscar pulls a small smartwatch from the drawer under the desk, along with a mobile phone.

"I've got a fucking phone," Reece snaps, appearing completely ungrateful and disappointed with his gift.

"Not one like this, Reece. This one has some amazing apps on it that perhaps only me and you will know how to work." Oscar speaks on level to Reece and Reece grins back at him. "One app, Reece, is very important. It's built into the watch as well." Hell, even Bren and I are intrigued, hanging on Oscar's every word.

"When you activate it, Reece, it allows you to use all cameras in the surrounding area. It also allows us to use the cameras in that area." Reece nods in understanding.

"Bet the fucker has a tracker in too, you fucking assholes!" Reece snipes, clutching the devices and leaving the room abruptly. No thank you in sight.

I'm going to have a receding hairline purely due to the stress of Reece!

"So did you know Reece knew Russian when you let him in here?" I ask.

"Not for sure, but I highly suspected." He smirks.

"What made you suspect that?"

"He'd spoken about Greg helping to train him and if I was choosing a language for a recruit, that's the one I would choose."

What Oscar says resonates with me. I sure as fuck don't like the thought of this prick Greg using my son as a recruit.

"Is that what you think? That this Greg is recruiting him?"

"No, I actually don't. If he was recruiting him, they'd both be with him now."

Oscar's response doesn't put me at ease any. I don't like that there's still so much we don't know and the uncertainty around this Greg is looming over us.

CHAPTER 13

Lily

I slept uneasily, knowing what lie ahead. I felt I was betraying Cal by what I was about to do and a sickening feeling overtakes me.

Last night Reece had informed me that Cal would be leaving in the morning to go to a meeting with some Russian or other. He told me this with a pointed look and I nodded in understanding.

I approached Sam at our front door and told him I needed someone to stay with Reece while I popped out for some shopping. He called Cal, who asked if it could wait. I explained to him it was for feminine products I needed to buy and I was desperate.

We agreed that Sam would stay with Reece while Jesse, the other bodyguard, drove me to the town pharmacy.

I tuck the burner phone in my purse and we head out.

We pull up to the pharmacy about twenty minutes later and I ask Jesse if he is joining me. He agrees to wait outside after scanning the store.

I walk into the store, kneeling to tie my shoelace. I take out the burner and text Greg to say I arrived. He replies for me to meet him at the fire exit in three minutes. I take a deep breath and glance toward Jesse, whose back is to the shop front.

I turn around and walk to the side of the store, confidently pushing open the employee door leading to the fire exit.

I sigh with relief, thanking my lucky stars for not being stopped by a staff member. I open the fire door and see Greg standing in the alley with his motorbike. I'm flooded with emotion and I fling my arms around his neck. He stumbles slightly before catching me and embracing me in a much-needed hug.

He puts me down. "We need to leave. Throw the burner." I nod.

I mount the bike and we speed off down the alley onto the main road, my stomach riddled with guilt.

CAL

I've felt anxious all day. I wasn't sure if it was to do with the meeting with Igor, as Bren suggested for my reason of being *off*.

The meeting went well. We'd beat the shit out of them as a warning and destroyed their warehouse with the help of a few grenades.

Finn had successfully uncovered our traitors at the docks. He'd brought them to the warehouse for a little Finn-ishing touch, as we called it. Otherwise known as pure torture. My brother was amazing with a knife.

But when I'd taken the call from Sam to say Lily wanted to go shopping, my instant reaction was to put a stop to it. I had a feeling something wasn't right. Lily had argued she needed fucking women's shit, so what could I say?

We're ten minutes out from the apartment when my phone rings. I glance at the screen to see it's Jesse calling. My stomach churns and my back straightens as I know instantly it's something to do with Lily.

Bren immediately senses my reaction and tells me to put it on speaker.

"Sir, we have a situation."

"Go on..." I prompt, an uneasy fury rising in me.

"I'm afraid it appears Lily has left the pharmacy without me. She erm... she appears to have left from the rear of the building on a motorbike."

I start shaking, rage flooding my veins. I want to smash the fucking phone. I want to rip Jesse's fucking stupid dickwad head off.

Bren takes the lead. "Are you sure she left on her own accord? She wasn't taken?"

Panic floods me. Oh fuck, was she taken?

"No, sir. I've already checked the surveillance tapes. She walked out the fire exit on her own accord, embraced the person waiting outside the door, threw a burner phone that I have retrieved, and mounted the motorbike on her own accord. Thirty minutes ago now, sir," he replies clearly.

She's fucking gone. Where the fuck has she gone? She's fucking left me.

I'm unaware of what happens and what is said next. I'm lost in my own mind and thoughts, but Bren takes over giving instructions.

As we enter the apartment, I'm shaking with desperation.

"Reece, come here please," Oscar calls loudly.

I'm pacing the apartment as Reece casually walks over to us, seemingly oblivious to my internal meltdown.

"Can you tell me who this man is talking to your mom?" he asks Reece, pointing at his tablet. I walk over to watch the footage of Lily hugging a tall ripped blonde dude. The bastard with a leather jacket was fucking built and they hugged like long-lost lovers. I feel fucking sick and betrayed.

"Yeah, that's just Greg, Mom's fuck buddy."

We all glare at Reece. I'm sure at that moment either one of us is prepared to snap and rip his fucking head off.

"Don't worry, she'll be back soon. She just needed to explain things to him."

"What do we do?" I ask Oscar in desperation.

"We wait," he replies.

Fuck. Fuck. Fuck. Fuck.

CHAPTER 14

Lily

As I make my way back up in the elevator, my stomach is tightening. I know I'm about to walk into an argument and honestly? I don't blame Cal for being pissed. I've completely gone behind his back and deceived him.

I take a deep breath as I open the door to the apartment. It's in darkness and eerily quiet.

"Nice of you to return," Cal calls from the couch where he's sitting, swirling his drink in his glass and causing the ice cubes to clink together. His posture is rigid and he's sitting with his legs open, elbows on his knees, facing the door. He's been waiting for me and I can cut the tension with a knife.

"Cal, I can explain..."

He pounces from his chair, slams his drink on the table, and flies toward me in rage, pushing me against the wall.

"Damn fucking right, you can explain, Lily. What the fuck are you playing at? Have you any idea how fucking worried I've been? Do you even fucking care?" His eyes search mine for an explanation.

I can't process his questions quickly enough. I gulp and shift my eyes with guilt. Cal senses it too, completely changing his course of questioning.

He takes a step back and looks at me from top to toe, looking for something. He meets my eyes and I see the rage and panic swirling inside them. He doesn't know whether to be pissed or hug me.

"Did you fuck him?" he spits out.

"What?" I gasp. Is he serious?

"Easy fucking question, Lily, did you fuck him?" he mocks. He's tugging his hair with nervousness and frustration. Fuck, is that what he thinks? I met Greg to sleep with him? Now I'm pissed. How dare he.

"No, Cal, I didn't fuck him," I choke out.

I'm playing with fire, I know I am, but fuck it. He's the one with the fiancée and yet he's trying to dictate to me? "Would it matter if I did?" I lift my chin defiantly.

"Yes, it fucking would matter, Lily," he bellows. "Of course, it fucking matters."

I sigh. This is getting us nowhere. "No, Cal, I didn't fuck Greg." He winces at Greg's name, clearly he's a sore spot for him. I get it. I understand he's jealous of another man having a relationship with me and his son, but that's in the past and he needs to realize that's where it's staying.

"I haven't slept with Greg in over a year," I say, meeting his eyes for reassurance.

His hand goes around my throat. It's not tight and I can sense it's a domineering action. He uses his thumb to stroke my jaw. "I can't bear the thought of someone touching you, Lily. You drive me so fucking crazy." He shakes his head, annoyed with himself. Slowly he rests his forehead against mine and takes shallow breaths as if to calm down. "I thought you were leaving me." His eyes are filled with sadness and desperation.

I close my eyes. I can feel the pain from his eyes seeping into me.

I palm my hand over his. "I don't want anyone else, Cal. I only want you."

Cal's whole body relaxes and I feel relieved that my words can take away his tension and hopefully give him some reassurance. His eyes are swimming with desire.

"Where's Reece?" I ask quickly, sensing the direction this is going.

Cal exhales and slowly takes a step back but doesn't release me. "He's downstairs with Oscar. They know you're back. Oscar's been keeping a look out on the cameras for you." His eyes swipe to the security monitors.

"I'm sorry I hurt you, Cal."

"You've no fucking idea, Lily." He shakes his head, his hurt visible.

"I know, and I know it doesn't mean much now, but I need you to know that was the only and last time I'll hold anything from you. I'll be completely honest from now on. No more secrets."

Cal looks surprised at that. "What makes you so sure about that? Why now?" His thumb brushes delicately over my jaw.

I look him in the eyes hoping he can see my truth. "Because I want what we've got to work. I don't want anything between us, Cal. I want to trust you and you need to trust me. I want you, Cal. I want us!"

I must have said the right thing because Cal pounces on me. His mouth clashes with mine, his hands are around my neck and pulling me closer. My hands go to his waist as our kiss becomes frenzied. My heart pounds, my nipples are tight and brushing against Cal's chest. He groans into my mouth and pushes his hard cock into me. "Don't tell me to stop, Lily. Please fuck, don't tell me to fucking stop," he pants.

He squeezes my ass and an appreciative sound bubbles from me. He lifts me by my ass and my legs wrap around his waist. He strides toward our bedroom and pushes the door open with my back before dropping me onto the bed. He's still attached to me as we both fumble with our clothes.

I lift my top over my head and Cal lets out a low carnal groan as he copies and pulls his top over his head. He makes quick work of removing my pants as I scramble to open his belt.

"Fuck, I wanted to take my time with you," he pants.

"I don't care, Cal, there's plenty of time. I just need you to fuck me, make me yours."

His eyes darken before pulling me into a punishing kiss. He kisses my face, neck, and chest as he opens his jeans and pushes them down, too desperate to remove them. I slide my panties to the side as he grabs his throbbing cock and pushes himself inside me.

Both of us are kissing and grabbing one another at a frantic pace, both desperate for a quick climax, clinging to one another for release.

I hold his head as he buries his face into my chest, pulling my tits out as he nips the swollen flesh. I push his ass down on me harder, loving the feel of him stretching me, pulling in and out. We fit together perfectly. We both gasp instantaneously, our bodies molding together for pleasure.

He pulls his body back, sitting on his knees, looking down at my open pussy as his cock thrusts into me. My legs spread open for him, his hands roaming my thighs as his cock thrusts in and out of me. His stomach muscles tense with the motion of his thrusts, the tightening of my pussy looming.

He watches our connected bodies before biting the inside of his mouth and exhaling to try and hold back his release.

"I'm so close, Cal. Fuck me faster. Harder," I pant out.

His eyes darken further and he watches me as I tug on my nipples. "Fuck, Lily, pull them fucking tighter baby, fucking come on my cock. I'm going to fill you up with my fucking come and you'll know who fucking owns you. Say it, say who fucking owns you!" His words are sharp and meaningful.

"You, Cal. You fucking own me," I scream as my orgasm rips through me with such intensity my head feels blurry. I've waited so long for this!

Cal follows behind me instantaneously, releasing a loud moan. His come floods my pulsing pussy and I've never felt anything so amazing and satisfying in my entire life.

We stay in the same position, looking at one another, embracing the connection neither of us wants to detach. Our chests pant in time with one another. Cal's mouth still open from his release, I pull him to me and kiss him as he falls onto his elbows, caging me in, securing me exactly where I want to be.

I lie in Cal's arms, on my side. Neither of us has spoken yet. I trail the hairs on his chest with my finger in a soothing circle.

"I should clean myself up," I chuckle as I start to rise.

Cal pulls me back down gently. "I don't want you to, I want you to sleep next to me with my come inside you, and then when I'm ready, I'm going to fuck you again and again to make sure you know who owns you."

I don't know why I find that such a turn-on, but I do. I stretch up to his lips and kiss him. "Good idea." I smile at him. His lips curve into a cocky smirk, pleased with my reply.

Cal's arm around me tightens a little. "I don't want you to see him again, Lily. Do you understand me?"

I fidget, biting my lip. I know I can't avoid it... "Greg's asked for a meeting with you and Oscar, he wants to talk to you both."

I look to his surprised eyes. I was expecting him to be angry, but he isn't, he's curious.

"Good, how do I contact him? I want to speak with him ASAP, Lily. I want this shit to stop hanging over us. I need us to move on." I nod in agreement.

I rise from the bed and walk to the closet. I pull out a burner phone from my jeans pocket and walk over to Cal, his body riddled with tension again. He's pissed at me, but I just raise an eyebrow. At least I'm being honest with this one!

"Call him and put it on fucking speaker," he snaps.

Greg answers on the second ring, his voice playful. "Hey, babe, miss me already?"

I wince and glance to Cal, whose jaw is tight and he's grinding his teeth in frustration. His eyes snap back up to me in aggravated annoyance.

"Greg, I've spoken to Cal and he's happy to meet you as soon as possible." I keep my tone even.

"Yeah, tell him I'll be there at ten in the morning." He cuts the call as Cal's about to speak, presumably to argue.

Cal throws his head back against the headboard, "I don't fucking believe this. He thinks he can just fucking stroll in here, into our fucking home, for what exactly?"

"He's not coming to cause trouble, Cal, I promise you.

He knows how I feel about you, at least you can ask him any questions you have." I shrug, looking down at my hands. "Me and Reece need closure, Cal. We need to sort this and then say goodbye." I nod to him. His eyes have spun to me and I swear he's going to argue but then he nods in agreement, relaxing my apprehension.

"Come sit up here, Lily." He pats his lap.

I straddle his waist. He brushes my hair behind my ears as he looks down my body in a loving, appreciative way, making me feel cherished. His eyes flare when he sees something on me, and I panic when I realize what he's seen.

He lifts me off him with ease, lying me down beside him as he crawls over and down my body to my scar just below my waist. He gently brushes his fingertips over the jagged scar, causing my body to break out in goosebumps and making me shudder.

"What happened?" His eyes meet mine in concern.

My eyes dart around and I can feel my chest tightening.

"Shh, it's okay, Lily. No secrets, remember?"

I look down to Cal, his eyes meet mine in understanding. He nods to encourage me as he gently kisses the scar.

"The baby..." My breathing is hitched as I struggle to form the words. "The baby, it's the scar from the baby, the stabbing." I shut my eyes tightly, trying to block the memories before they invade me.

Cal stops moving, stilling as I speak the words. He slowly crawls up to me at the top of the bed, lying beside me again and stroking my hair. "He stabbed you?"

I nod my head and wince at the thought.

"He meant to harm you then? It wasn't an accident?" he questions.

"The argument, it got out of control," I gulp as I try to

explain not wanting to relive the day, the day that I felt like my life had been destroyed.

"He was enraged and wouldn't listen to me, he was screaming and throwing things, cutlery, plates, anything. He was completely out of control, Cal. He'd never been like that before, never. I wouldn't have ever had that around Reece."

I open my eyes to look at him, I need him to know I wasn't some damsel in distress, or someone scared of an abusive partner. "He never lifted a finger to me, not once, not until that day."

"What happened that day? Why was that day different?" His eyebrows pull together trying to decipher the events.

I laugh slightly. "Reece happened that day. They'd had shipments go missing, believe it or not. They tracked the computer to one used inside our house, and low and behold the only people in the house at the time were me... and Reece."

Cal pulls back slightly to look at me in concern.

"Nico didn't know of Reece's capabilities." I blow out a breath. "Jeez neither did I until then. He'd not yet learned how to cover his tracks. Nico assumed it was me. I wasn't going to tell him otherwise, not when he was so enraged, but I wanted to try and talk him down." I shake my head, remembering how he wouldn't listen to rhyme nor reason.

"His eyes—they cut straight through me, as though he couldn't see me anymore. As though I was nothing to him. He wasn't going to listen to reason, he wasn't prepared to look for an alternative. In his mind, I'd done what his father and brother had always said I'd do—betray him.

"I had the knife in my hand from chopping the salad. I was backed up to the kitchen counter and he was screaming at me, in my face. His eyes were so wild, he was calling me all the names his father and brother accused me of. He'd completely gone—he wasn't Nico anymore. Plates were being thrown and he kept lunging forward. I screamed at him to stop. He backhanded me and I couldn't stop shaking. I started walking toward him. I felt broken, he'd never hurt me before, I couldn't stop shaking, and his eyes darted to the knife. I don't know whether he thought I was going to use it or if he wanted to use it but he lunged for it. We tussled and he grabbed my throat as I was kicking and screaming at him to stop and listen to me. The next thing I knew, a sharp pain gripped me and I choked."

I swallow thickly, overcome with emotion. "His face, he looked so fucking broken and shocked, he looked at me as if he didn't recognize me. I looked down and it was as though time had slowed down. I saw the puddle of blood on the floor from between my legs before I saw the blood on my top." I pant, struggling to get the words out to Cal, yet desperate to get the whole story out before I'm too upset and have to stop.

"Nico crumbled to the floor before me. He just fell with a wail. A sickening wail." I close my eyes as Cal gently brushes the tears from my cheeks, nuzzling loving and encouragingly into my hair.

"How far along were you?" he asks gently.

"Twenty-three weeks." I shake my head and lick my lips, looking up to the ceiling to compose myself.

"It was the worst day of my life, Cal. I lost so much that day."

"You're so strong, Lily, so fucking strong. Do you hear me? I know you've been through hell but I'm here for you now. I'm so fucking proud of you, baby." He embraces me, kissing my head, and rubbing soothing hands through my hair as I openly sob into his chest. I cling to him.

CHAPTER 15

Cal

I wait for Lily to fall asleep before moving. I gently pull the sheet over her and kiss her forehead.

I'm so proud of Lily but I can't help but not be sorry about the events that happened in her past, without them they wouldn't have led her back to me. I know that makes me a bastard, but I wouldn't have my family now if it wasn't for those events. Of course, hearing her relive her trauma was hard and I felt the devastation alongside Lily. I wanted to erase her pain and kill the prick for hurting her so deeply.

I move to the kitchen and make some business calls after speaking to Oscar, who assures me Reece is fine and is happy to stay overnight with him.

Oscar is keen to have the meeting with Greg. Although I hadn't originally wanted Lily and Reece there, I know it's the right thing to do. She is right, they do need closure.

I wake with a jump. After setting my alarm for 8:00 a.m.,

it still shocks me when it goes off. I'd wanted to be up and ready for this prick to come and fuck off out of our lives forever.

I still feel uneasy. I feel Lily is going to change her mind and choose him over me. I can't help the niggling doubt inside my head that's making me so damn insecure and jealous. It isn't a feeling I'm familiar with, so I'm completely uneasy and I feel fucking completely overwhelmed.

It must have become obvious, because Lily sits up and hovers over me, brushing my hair from my forehead. "Hey, what's the matter?"

I shrug in response, completely aware of how childlike I'm acting.

"Are you worried about this morning?"

My eyes must hold some emotional unease.

"You've nothing to be afraid of Cal, I promise."

She closes her lips around mine and I relax into her.

Slowly she moves down the bed, kissing my chest and hips along the way. She glances back up at me, darting her tongue over my pelvis, causing me to thrust. My chest is tightening with anticipation as I kick the sheets off from around me.

Lily's tongue darts over the tip of my already hard cock and she suckles the tip with her lips gently, causing me to moan. Fuck she's incredible!

She widens her mouth over the head of my cock, sucking and licking before releasing me.

"Fuck, Lily, you've no idea how fucking turned on I am right now."

She trails kisses up and down my cock, tormenting me. She gently plays with my balls, tugging them lightly while licking up the outside of my length and back down the other side. I push my hips up toward her as encouragement. Fuck, I need her greedy mouth around me.

I exhale and give in to my thoughts. "Suck my fucking cock, Lily," I demand through gritted teeth.

She places her hands around the base as she moves her mouth over the top and slowly slips her mouth down, completely ignoring my demand. Jesus, it's torture!

Climbing inside my legs, she moves her hands to my thighs, covering my cock with her wet mouth as she thrusts up and down, her juicy fucking lips dripping. I'm so fucking turned on. She's using her mouth to fuck me, not me fucking her.

I sit up a little more to look down on her better, put my hands on her head, and gently tug her hair as she nods in silent agreement. I work her head up and down, in complete control now, just how I fucking like it. I fuck her gorgeous face. The thrill runs through my veins and into my cock as I work my hips to match the pull of her hair. She moans around my cock and the vibrations ripple around me.

"Fuck, baby, just like that. Keep your fucking tongue doing that. Fuck, baby, I'm gonna come soon. You gonna swallow me down like a good girl?"

She nods and that's all I need to tip me over the edge as I fuck her face with vigor and roar my release.

I throw myself back on my bed, chuckling. "Jesus, that was fucking incredible, baby. You can wake me up like that every fucking day."

She pops her head up and gives me a coy smile that shoots through me. She's so fucking beautiful. So fucking mine.

"Come on. We best get you showered, then get ready for that prick to get here," I say, reaching out my hand.

"Let's see if I can make you come in my shower all over my fingers, beautiful."

Her eyebrows raise in a silent challenge. Game fucking on, beautiful.

CHAPTER 16

Lily

We ate breakfast after Cal decided to eat me out in the shower. I'm not complaining, the man is incredible. My legs still feel shaky.

I'm sitting nervously in the living area with Reece bouncing about like an excitable puppy, oblivious to the tension.

Bren's and Cal's backs are straight and tense. They're sitting on one end of the couch and Oscar is in full-blown business mode with his tablet at the table, while we wait for Greg to arrive. I'm on the other side of the couch and can't stop nibbling my fingernails and messing with my hands between my legs, anxiety wavering from me.

There's a knock at the door. My heart sinks as Sam opens it. "Sir, he's just coming up the elevator now."

"Send him straight in," Cal snaps. I breathe and will Cal to remain calm, knowing full well Greg will toy with him if he exposes his weaknesses.

There's a tap and Reece jumps up as Greg comes

through the door, filling the doorway with his muscular body. Cal's eyes dart to mine and I smile at him for reassurance.

"Jacob, come here man," Greg calls to Reece as Reece almost knocks him over in a bear hug.

I feel the guys' sharp glaring eyes on me as I look up from bowing my head and calmly stand to walk over to Greg.

Cal stands and steps toward me.

"Abi, come here, babe." Yep, I could fucking kill Greg right now.

Cal's step is stunted at Greg's words. I continue walking toward him, stepping up to kiss the side of his cheek. I feel his arm about to band around me so I step out of his hold before he can embrace me. He laughs and holds an eyebrow up in question.

"Don't fucking start. Greg, please," I snap and walk back to Cal. Cal's face has gone from hurt to relieved in a split second.

I kiss Cal gently on his lips. His shoulders loosen from their tight hold as he bands his arms around to hold me in place with him. He whispers to me, "Thank you, baby."

Reece is talking a mile a minute to Greg, who hasn't made it much farther into the room.

Greg raises his voice sternly, putting his hand up in front of Reece. "Jacob, shut the fuck up a minute and give me a chance to think. Jesus, man you're like a fucking yapping Chihuahua."

Bren laughs at Greg while standing. "Do you want a drink, Greg?"

"Yeah, beer thanks."

Bren starts to gather everyone's drinks.

"So, who's the dick in charge of security here?" Greg

asks, glaring at Oscar and knowing full well who oversees security. I roll my eyes. Here we go...

"Problem?" Oscar snaps as his eyes sharpen on Greg, scrutinizing Greg's appearance.

"Yeah, your metal detection and security procedures are shit. They searched me and failed twice," he says while holding two fingers up, laughing while enjoying Oscar's intense stare.

"How so?" Oscar drawls.

Greg kicks one boot next to the other and out pops the base of his boot. Bending down to it, he pulls out a small knife. He holds one finger up while throwing the knife on the counter for emphasis.

He holds up a second finger. Moving around his back, he lifts his belt, revealing a small pocket where he pulls out another knife, throwing that down as well.

He then decides to completely shame Oscar by holding out another finger, causing Oscar to curse under his breath, clearly pissed at Greg.

Greg digs his hands into his jeans, moving down to his balls. He raises an eyebrow, looking directly at me with the silent taunt. Cal's hands tighten on me, without realizing.

Of course, I know Greg and I know he's a cocky prick that likes to make a statement and play games. If it means he can embarrass someone or bump his own ego he will do it happily.

Out he pulls a fucking grenade! He's laughing now, as he places it on the countertop. Bren and Cal glare at Oscar accusingly.

Oscar pays no attention to the growing tension. "Point made," he snaps, averting his eyes from Greg and back to his tablet.

Greg settles on the couch with the beer as I sit alongside

Cal. He opens his backpack and pulls out a thick manila file, throwing it onto the coffee table in front of me and Cal. "What's this?" Cal asks.

He waves his hand at the file. "That's everything—all documentation, original IDs, medical documents, certifications, everything basically to do with them," he says while looking at me.

Cal leans forward, opening the front page. He shuffles uncomfortably as he reads the first page aloud. "Abigail Lillian Price and Jacob Reece Price." He looks at me in confusion.

Greg clears his throat. "I made them use their middle names after the Nico incident," he explains.

Cal looks to me for clarification. "I'm Lily. I'm not Abi anymore and neither is Reece Jacob anymore." He nods in understanding and his shoulders loosen, the tic in his jaw slacking.

Oscar speaks up. "Can you tell us how you met Lily? She's been reluctant to speak about you."

"Good girl." He laughs, making me roll my eyes. "I met Abi—sorry—Lily while working as a lieutenant for Nico Garcia. I was first on scene the day the incident occurred."

"You mean the day he tried to kill Lily and killed her baby?" Cal snaps. I tighten my hand in his.

Greg rubs his jaw. "Yes. Like I said, I was the first on the scene. I took her to the hospital. That was the last time I had contact with Nico."

"What was Nico doing while you did this? Is he looking for them?" Bren asks.

"Nico was slumped on the floor in a shocked state. He grabbed my wrist as I scooped Lily up. He whispered Jacob's name to me, looking me in the eye and nodding once. I knew that was him asking me to collect Jacob from school and deal with them both."

"When you say deal with them both, what do you mean?" Cal says as his body tightens.

Greg lifts his hands in defense. "Not that, I can assure you!"

"How? How can you be sure he didn't expect you to kill them?"

Greg shakes his head. "Regardless of what you think of Nico, he loved them. Both of them. He went against his father and brother on numerous occasions for Lily and Reece and until that day, he completely stood up to them. I honestly don't know what changed.

"If he wanted Lily dead, he'd have done it or got someone else to do it. He wouldn't have asked me to get Jacob from school. He did that knowing I'd get them both to safety. He asked me, knowing my capabilities hiding and protecting them. I've intel inside the house and I'm assured he hasn't even tried looking for me or them."

"When you say, take them to safety, safety from who?" Oscar asks.

Greg looks at me and I know I'm not going to like his answer. I close my eyes and wait for it.

"Safety from Raul Garcia Senior and his heir Raul junior, Nico's older and more deranged brother. They're the real threat, not Nico. I can't say either way if they're actively searching for them, but if I had to guess I'd say abso-fucking-lutely."

I shudder at Greg's words. The thought of either of them finding me or Reece terrifies me. Cal pulls me closer to him and places a loving kiss on my head.

"Why would they need safety from them?" Bren asks.

Greg shakes his head and laughs slightly in disbelief,

throwing his hand in Reece's direction. "Because our little hacker whiz over here stole some cargo from them. Isn't that right, Reece?"

Reece jumps up from the couch, temper erupting. "Here we fucking go again. I told you I wouldn't do it again, didn't I?"

"Yet you hacked your family's accounts to withdraw funds," Oscar replies.

"Fuck you, Oscar. I didn't say I wouldn't hack, just that I wouldn't steal anyone's cargo, moody fucking pricks! Trying to stop me from hacking, what a fucking joke. I haven't done anything wrong, I'm only fucking looking!"

We ignore Reece's theatrics and mumblings. "What's done is done now, Reece. I'm simply explaining how we got here," Greg says, waving his hands at Reece as though he's an annoying gnat.

"So they're pissed about the cargo going missing? Are they still pissed?" Cal asks.

"Absolutely, I'm afraid. They're convinced Lily has the knowledge of where the cargo is."

"Can't we just give it back? Reece knows where it is, right?" Cal suggests, shooting his eyes toward Reece.

Greg shakes his head. "I've suggested we don't do that. If we return the cargo there's no leverage over them. There's no reason they wouldn't dispose of Lily and Reece. If you withhold the cargo, you will always have the upper hand if a problem arises. As of yet, no threat toward them has been made. However, the Garcias do not forget, and my understanding of the cargo is that it's something valuable to them. How you choose to handle this is your guys' call but it's worked out for us so far." Greg relaxes against the couch.

Cal sits back thinking. "What's inside the cargo? Any ideas?" Oscar asks.

Greg shrugs. "I'm guessing files, documents they don't want anyone seeing, ledgers maybe?"

"Where is the cargo?" Bren asks abruptly, asking an obvious question that none of us have asked.

Greg shrugs. "I don't know. Nobody but Reece knows and I told him to keep it that way. I wanted Lily and Reece to trust me and therefore there's no reason for me to know."

Cal nods at this and if I'm not mistaken, he seems quite impressed. His eyes dart to Oscar's.

"So, what happens now?" Cal asks.

"Now I leave these two with you guys—they're your family." Greg stands to leave and turns pointedly. "But if you ever hurt either of them, I will hunt you fucking down and gut you." He grins manically.

The guys stand. Cal moves forward and offers his hand to Greg. "Thank you for taking such good care of them both."

Greg shakes his hand and nods. "Lily, walk me down, please?"

I jump up and Cal glares at me. "I'll be two minutes, I promise!"

He nods reluctantly.

Reece gives Greg a hug goodbye as we exit the apartment together.

CAL

As soon as Greg and Lily step foot in the elevator, Oscar and I are in the den and have the footage of them on the screen.

"This is goodbye then?" Lily asks, with her head downcast and shifting awkwardly from foot to foot.

"It is." Greg sounds glum in response and looks down at Lily. "They care about you, Lily. I can see that they'll keep you safe. You need to trust them and be honest with them. I can see Cal is fiercely protective of you both."

Oscar and I look to one another and both raise our eyebrows. I guess we hadn't realized Greg was rooting for us, for our family.

"Make sure Reece keeps up with his studies, languages specifically, and make sure Oscar keeps tabs on him. He's a fucking disaster waiting to happen." Greg laughs to himself. Lily nods her head awkwardly as Greg sighs. He aims his eyes to the camera and then back at Lily. He fidgets in his pocket and in a split second the camera feed cuts off.

"What the fuck just happened?" I erupt.

"Calm down. He's cut the feed, blocked it somehow. I should be able to override whatever he's just done. It'll be back up and running in a second." Oscar is tapping furiously at the keyboard.

"Hurry the fuck up, Oscar, that's more than a few fucking seconds!"

The screen flicks back on. They've reached the ground floor and Greg steps out of the elevator, winks to the camera, and starts fastening his belt. I'm going to kill the fucker!

I jump from my seat. Steam must be billowing out my ears and my face is on fire with rage.

"Calm the fuck down. He's just winding you up, Cal. Jesus, you're so fucking easy to wind up. Here, this should make you feel better, I've retrieved the footage."

I settle back into my chair reluctantly.

"Look at me, Lily..." Greg says, pulling her into a hug. "You're both going to be fine. I'll be leaving the country for a while, but you know how to reach me if you need me."

"I won't need you, that's the thing. It's goodbye and..." she sniffles "... thank you, Greg, for everything. I'll never forget everything you've done for us. I'll never forget you."

He bends down. No, he better fucking not—

He kisses her cheek and smells her hair, as if to commit her scent to memory. "Take care, Abi," he says, clearing his throat as he turns away from her. He tugs at his belt and straightens his slumped shoulders with a smirk on his face. Fucker!

CHAPTER 17

Lily

The rest of the day is uneventful. Cal spends the afternoon fussing around me. He knows I'm feeling down, and he's being very sweet when I'd expected him to be annoyed. I'm grateful for his compassion. I never knew a man could be so loving and thoughtful.

"Hey, I've run you a bath," he announces as I'm clearing away the plates from dinner. Reece is in his room on his devices that Oscar is acutely monitoring.

I walk to the bathroom and smile to myself. Bubbles are overflowing the tub.

Cal touches my shoulders. "Fancy sharing?" he asks with mischief dancing in his eyes.

He gently pulls my top over my head, sucking in his breath as he reaches behind my back to open my bra. His eyes are heavy with lust. He gulps. "So fucking beautiful."

Cal tugs my pants down my legs and I step out of them. He slowly rises to his feet, drinking in my body as he stands.

He curves his fingertips around my panty waistband and lowers them, gently kissing my short delicate curls.

Cal takes my hand and walks me to the bathtub. He helps me in and the water rises to my breasts. He never takes his eyes from me. He locks the door and faces me with a smirk that makes me laugh. Mmm, this is not going to be a clean bath, that's for sure.

Cal strips his clothes off in no time. His huge cock bobs as he strides toward me. I lean forward for him to lower himself into the bath behind me.

The water flows over the bathtub as he settles down with his legs wrapped around me, my back to his front. I lean back against his hard chest and sigh.

Picking up a sponge and soap, Cal rubs them together and creates a lather. He gently brushes the lather over my neck, followed by a kiss there, then over my shoulders, followed by a kiss there. Everywhere he cleans he kisses afterward.

"I feel the fucking need to suck your skin into my mouth and mark you all over. I'm like a fucking horny teenager when I'm around you, wanting to stake my claim." His laugh is deep but he also sounds pissed with himself for being so possessive.

"Well, I kinda like you being all territorial." I smile.

He lathers my breasts. My chest rises and falls as he gently plays with my nipples, circling them and toying with them, turning them into sharp buds. I fidget, rubbing myself against him as I'm getting more and more turned on.

"You like that, baby? So fucking beautiful. My cock's rock hard for you," Cal pants.

He tips my head back to rest on his shoulder. I can look him in his eyes in this position. They're hooded, flitting between looking at me and then back to my breasts. I open my legs in encouragement.

"Play with yourself, Lily. Let me see you."

I move my hands to my pussy and move the wetness toward my clit, gently rubbing circles as Cal continues to play with my nipples.

"Fuck, Cal, you turn me on so much," I pant. "Please..."

"Please what, baby? Tell me what you want."

"I want you to fill me up, Cal. Put your cock in me and come inside me."

Cal releases a strangled moan. "Ah, fuck I love your dirty fucking mouth. Sit on my cock, baby." He lifts my ass and I hover above him. He eases me down onto him. We exhale together when he enters me. I slowly shift from side to side to loosen myself around him in this position. "You good?" He pants.

I nod. His hands tighten on my breasts, becoming almost painful but it's pleasurable all the same—a perfect combination of pain and pleasure.

Cal tugs at my nipples, drawing them tighter. I rise up and down on his cock. Water sloshes out of the tub, over-flowing onto the floor.

Cal's pace speeds up while squeezing my breasts together. "Fuck baby, look at you, your fucking tits, amazing!" His mouth goes to my shoulder and he sucks hard, drawing the skin between his teeth, causing me to moan and tighten around him as I get closer to my orgasm.

Cal can feel the constricting of my pussy and he tightens his hold on my chest as he drives into me harder and faster. "Fuck, almost fucking there." He roars his release. His cock pulsing inside me sends me over the edge. I come, screaming his name.

CAL

It's been an amazing week having Lily and Reece in the apartment with me. Reece started school on Monday and settled in well. Both he and Lily were mortified that I insisted on taking him in to meet the principal on his first day but after explaining this was my first time doing a school run, they both relaxed and accommodated my anxieties.

It's Friday night and I've just made love to Lily, in our bed. I'd been given orders to only come in when Reece was asleep and I had to be up and out before he was awake, which was a load of shit, but I understood she wanted the Penelope situation sorted before we came clean to Reece about our full relationship status.

Lily lies beside me, twirling the few chest hairs I have around her fingers. "So dinner with your parents tomorrow, who will be there?"

"All my brothers and obviously Ma and Da. Uncle Don may show his face but I'm not sure."

"Tell me about Connor and Finn. I don't know much about them."

I breathe out. "Okay, so Finn is the bad boy of the family. He went into the army and came out with a bigger attitude than before he went in. He's definitely the one with the shortest fuse. Connor is probably most like me in appearance and personality, softer than our brothers but very much a playful bachelor." I laugh describing my brothers.

"How come none of your brothers have married? Do they have girlfriends? Fiancées?"

I chuckle. "Absolutely not. So, Bren has not got the time nor patience for a woman in his life. I mean, you've seen him. He's fucking so serious, he probably sleeps with his gun in his hand. No fucking softy there. If he wants a date, he'd pay for one, if he wants sex..." I shrug. "Maybe he pays for that too. Fuck knows, but he doesn't date.

"Finn had a girlfriend before he went in the army. She was the complete opposite of him, very sweet and innocent. Anyway, he went into the army, she was pissed off and left him to live with her family on the West Coast. Last I heard she'd married someone. He has more women than dinners, some last longer than others but not often. He soon gets bored and trades them in."

Lily sighs. "That's sad. Everyone deserves to be happy. What about Connor and Oscar?"

I kiss her nose. "I know, baby, but not everyone wants the whole family thing. I think that's why I was the one burdened with the engagement. I was probably the best candidate of a bad bunch. Anyway, Oscar, well you've seen him. He can hardly bear anyone touching him and he's very secretive. Finn is forever messing with him, saying he'll be the forty-year-old virgin."

Lily looks up at me. "Do you think he is?"

I laugh, shaking my head. "No, I don't. I've seen the fucking condoms in his room and I could have sworn I heard a woman in his bedroom once when I let myself in. He wasn't fucking happy and now he has to buzz us in to enter. I'm surprised he lets Reece in his apartment. He barely lets us across the threshold."

Lily laughs. "I hope he finds someone who cares deeply for him. When he falls for someone, it's going to be hard for him."

"Yeah, you're right. He deserves to be happy. When I look at him, I can't help but see an older Reece. It's certainly made me realize how much Oscar has been dealing with, with very little help and support. Not to mention my da, who thinks Oscar is a freak." I shake my head, utterly ashamed of my father's previous words and actions toward Oscar. I'd given him a stern talking to again this week about meeting Reece. I didn't want him making the same mistakes with him as he has with Oscar.

"So, Connor, he had a love of his life when he was young but pretty much refused to admit how much she meant to him, even though it was ridiculously obvious to us all. They had a fight of some sort—he wouldn't share the details— and next thing we know, she's disappeared and her family refused to pass any details on to him. He was a dumbass back then and probably treated her like shit. Anyway, he sulked for what seemed like forever before becoming New Jersey's very own playboy."

"So, he loved and lost. Poor Connor. Where did she disappear to, do you know?"

"Nope. Like I said, her family were all hush-hush. Her dad was an asshole and very strict with her, so basically she and Connor would sneak around. I imagine they sent her to live with family or a fucking nunnery or something. She was best off away from her father and brother, they were controlling pricks. They dabbled in dealing drugs on the streets, brother fancies himself as a big-time dealer. Anyway, in general not nice people." I shake my head thinking about how such a nice girl came from such a shitty family, but then I look down to Lily and realize that's exactly what she came from. I kiss her head protectively.

"Connor was the one who actually encouraged me not to stop searching for you. I guess he saw some of his own hurt in what I was dealing with."

"Well at least I know a little more about them, but I'm so freaking nervous about meeting your dad, Cal," she admits.

"Don't be, Lily. Seriously, he's going to spout a loud of shit that we're completely used to. He's an arrogant ass. Anything to do with Reece, I'll sort. Oscar and Bren have your backs as will Finn and Con, you'll see. Plus, Ma can't wait to meet you both." She sighs into my chest. I wrap my arm around her to bring her closer, kissing her head gently.

CHAPTER 18

Lily

We pull up to the back of the huge estate of Cal's family home. The grounds surrounding the property are beautifully maintained. The house is grand but has a cottagey feel to it, with vines running up the outside and neatly tamed flowered borders. I look over the perfectly manicured lawns and imagine a handful of young boys running around the gardens, a smile adorns my lips.

Reece insisted on bringing Puss with him. He's clearly agitated because the poor cat has not been put down and looks close to being throttled. Cal cuts the engine and looks to me. "It'll be fine, I promise." His hands are entwined with mine and he squeezes them in a sweet gesture.

He leans in and kisses me. This is the first time he's kissed me in front of Reece and once he realizes what he's doing, he quickly pulls away and glances at Reece. I sit wide-eyed and shocked, but after glancing at Reece, I realize he's oblivious. Relief runs through me.

We get out of the car and Cal comes around to my side and pulls me closer to him, throwing his other arm over Reece's shoulder. Cal's spine straightens and he walks with a sense of pride.

Reece doesn't shy away from Cal's affection. If anything, he seeks it as a way of comfort. Cal looks to me with a raised eyebrow, delight written all over his gorgeous face. I smile back at him. It feels like quite the achievement with Reece.

Cal lifts his head and strides forward. Before he reaches the door, it's flung open and out comes a woman in her early to mid-sixties, dark hair with flecks of gray pulled up into a messy ponytail. She has an apron around her waist and a smile on her face. As we approach, I notice her eyes are a beautiful light shade of blue. She quickly wipes her hands on her apron.

"Ma, this is Lily and Reece."

"Nice to meet you, Lily. I'm Cynthia, but please call me Cyn. Hello, Reece." Cal's mother greets us politely with a genuine soft smile.

"Nice to meet you, Cyn. Thank you so much for having us over for dinner. Reece, say hello," I prompt Reece, but he's fidgeting nervously, scowling with his head hung low, nuzzling Puss.

Cal looks to his mother and shakes his head gently.

"Oh Reece, I love cats. What a beauty!" she declares, walking slowly toward Puss with her hand out to stroke the cat.

Reece's head shoots up. "I fucking love this cat!" he spits.

She laughs gently and nods in agreement. "I can see why, such a beauty," she coos.

I smile in Cyn's direction, grateful for her gentle efforts with Reece. It's very sweet that she's trying to settle him.

Cal leads us inside, with Reece following behind as Cyn continues trying to coax a conversation from him.

We walk into a big open-plan kitchen with a huge wooden table in the middle. The table is already set and Bren is sitting next to his father, who is at the head of the table. Oscar is sitting nearest to us and the farthest away from his father, meaning Oscar will be sitting next to his mother.

My heart sinks for Oscar. There's an obvious void in the father-son relationship.

Bren stands as we enter, his large muscled body blocking the light. "Hey, Lily. Beer?"

I nod with a smile in response. "Thanks, Bren."

Cal's father rises from the table. He's huge! He's Bren's size, with wide shoulders, although they are slightly hunched and showing his age a little. He has dark hair, small strips of silver running through, with an obvious wave to it, and piercing blue eyes. Wow. No wonder all the men in the family have blue eyes. Their mother's are a soft blue and their father's a strong blue. There's no disputing where the men get their looks from.

"Ah, so this is the little vixen that's stolen my son's heart, eh?" the father chuckles to himself.

I almost choke. "Erm, nice to meet you. I'm Lily." I hold out my hand. He takes it and shakes it hard with authoritative confidence.

"Nice to meet you, Lily. I'm Brennan. Thanks for joining us."

I nod in response and look to Cal. His eyes hold a laser-hard focus on his father as if to say, "I'm watching every word."

I catch his eye and he smiles softly before scowling back at his father.

Cal sits next to his father and encourages me to sit next to him with Reece on the other side next to Oscar, putting Reece farther from Cal's father.

"What the feck is that thing?" Brennan bellows, looking in Reece's direction.

Reece's head shoots up and before Cal can respond, he snaps back at Brennan, "It's a fucking cat. Are you that fucking stupid?"

I tense. I need someone to make me disappear. Everyone stops and holds their breath. Brennan sucks in a sharp breath and then he absolutely belly laughs, his shoulders shaking.

We all visibly relax. Reece is murmuring under his breath, "Fucking stupid thick fucking cunt, old bastard, not a fucking dog, is it? No, not a dog, are you Puss?"

Small conversations of chatter are filling the dining area as we wait for Finn and Connor to arrive. Oscar is engaging with Reece, who's slowly starting to relax.

The door flies open and in breeze the brothers, one in a leather jacket and one in a cap back to front. The latter stops and kisses his mother on the cheek. She laughs gently and brushes him off.

"Where the fuck have you pair been?" Brennan barks, his aggression cutting through the room.

"Traffic," the leather jacket one grumbles and rolls his eyes. He has sharp features with a few scars on his face, soft blue eyes, and short-cropped hair that make it impossible to tell if he has the same waves as Cal and Reece. He's arrogantly chewing a toothpick and throws himself lazily into the chair opposite me.

He winks at me. I spare a glance toward Cal from the corner of my eye to see Cal shooting a venomous glare aimed back toward him.

Cal flings his hand toward him in explanation. "Lily this is Finn. Finn, Lily."

I smile back at him, just managing a "hi" before the next body drops in the chair beside Finn, opposite Reece.

"This is Connor." Connor is a younger version of Cal, just more muscular and slightly broader.

He's gorgeous but holds an aura around him that makes it obvious to everyone that he knows how gorgeous he is. He's most definitely a charmer.

Connor smiles a dazzling eye-twinkling smile. "Nice to meet you, beautiful!" His eyes quickly cut from me to Reece. "Wow, fuck, Cal, he is a mini-you," he says, looking at Reece in awe.

Reece glares in response and makes a hissing noise. His eyes drill into Connor.

Brennan's abrupt roar makes me jump. "What the feck is that on your head, Con?"

"A cap, Da," Connor replies in a lazy cocky tone, rolling his eyes at his father's question.

"Take it off at the fucking dinner table, shithead. I can see it's a fucking cap, smug little bastard," Brennan bellows back, banging his fist on the table. The cutlery jumps in response.

Cal's softly drawing circles on my leg under the table, to calm me but I'm not sure whose benefit it's more for.

Connor pulls his cap from his head and brushes a hand through his thick messy wavy dark hair.

Finn sits slumped in his chair with a can't-be-bothered attitude. He removes the toothpick, pointing it as he speaks, "So Reece, what's the cat's name?"

Oscar sits straighter. "Leave him the fuck alone, Finn, you've been warned!" He pokes a finger in Finn's direction.

Finn chuckles to himself and holds his hands up in defense.

Reece shoots Finn a glare. "Name's Pussy."

Both Connor and Finn look at one another and crack up laughing like little schoolboys. I roll my eyes.

"You called your cat Pussy?" Connor asks, a huge cheeky smile on his face, struggling to contain his laugh.

"Yes, are you fucking deaf?"

They both look at one another and snigger again. "Your kid's hilarious, Cal. He's all serious and shit just like you!"

"Calm it, Finn," Cal shoots back. He's getting visibly annoyed and agitated.

"Jesus, you're so fucking uptight. I hope you're managing to loosen him up a little, Lily," Finn jokes, wiggling his eyebrows.

"Yeah, and I'm sure Pussy helps loosen him up too." Con splutters at his own joke.

Oh my god, it's like being with a couple of teenagers. I can't help but smile at their childishness. I bite my lip to stifle my laugh.

Reece is not happy. "You stupid fucking pricks!" He sneers back.

Finn sits up with a smile on his face. Leaning forward he whispers, "Does Da like Pussy, Reece?"

Bren hits him at the back of the head, hard! His smile drops and he holds his hands up again in defense, scowling at Bren.

Reece is not done. "Fucking everybody likes Pussy!" he chimes.

At that, everyone starts laughing, it's hard not to. There's only Reece that is now sitting there with a scowl on his face, completely unaware of his words.

Cyn begins bringing the food out. I'd offered to help her

but she refused. To be honest, she clearly enjoys waiting on her boys, she has such soft approach with them but with a stern edge.

Connor and Finn need keeping in line and now and again she shoots them a look that settles them or clips Connor around the ear for him talking inappropriately with Finn. I instantly warm to her and her soft maternal smile.

Just when everyone starts helping themselves to the food and passing it around the table, Reece pipes up, "Why've you set a plate at that chair?" He points to the empty place. Silence descends.

"That's a place we set for Keenan, buddy. He passed away, but we always set a place for him," Cal gently explains.

"Well, that's fucking stupid, why do that when he's not here?"

Oh god, please make me invisible! The table once again falls silent, all eyes on Reece.

I clear my throat to explain. "It's a sign of respect, Reece. Some people choose to do that to include their loved ones in their day-to-day lives."

"Well, that's fucking stupid. Do you put food on his plate too?" He chuckles, completely misunderstanding the whole respect thing.

Finn cracks up laughing his cocky laugh. Shoving his toothpick back in his mouth, pushing it from side to side, enjoying every awkward moment.

I lean closer to Reece and look at him pointedly. "That's a redcars Reece, do you understand me?"

Reece nods firmly in acknowledgment, dipping his head and gently tugging his hair in frustration

"I'm sorry about that everyone," I apologize, completely embarrassed.

"It's fine," Cal replies while putting his hand in mine.

We all continue to pass the food and chatter.

"Do you like sports, Reece?" Connor asks.

"No, I fucking don't. It's fucking pointless."

Cyn walks behind Reece and leans over him to retrieve the empty water jug. She puts her arm onto Reece's shoulder to balance herself, but he jumps in response to her touch.

"I'm so sorry, honey," she apologizes just as quickly.

Finn raises a curious eyebrow at Cal. "He's like Oscar, he doesn't like to be touched." Cal quickly explains.

Reece shoots Oscar a confused glare. "Well that's a fucking lie, you like being touched."

Oscar looks back at him with a matching confused expression, then he looks to Cal and me for an explanation. I shrug, just as confused.

Reece sighs and rolls his eyes, clearly annoyed at having to explain. "What about those fucking prostitutes you pay to come into your apartment? They must touch you. Isn't that the point to them?"

My eyes bug out, shell-shocked. Con chokes on his water. I scan the table, shock and mortification on everyone's faces. Finn bursts out laughing and poor Oscar sits there in utter disbelief.

"Enough, Reece, fucking redcars," I sneer into his ear.

Oscar puts his head down to continue eating and ignores everyone's stares but he's clearly uncomfortable. Obviously he doesn't want to elaborate.

Finn sits up straighter in his chair and leans over the table toward Oscar in a taunting position.

He has a smug grin on his face and won't remove his eyes from Oscar while eating.

Clearly, he's awaiting an explanation. Connor sits sniggering at Finn's taunting demeanor.

Bren speaks up in a sharp, stern voice, "Finn, enough!"

"Just wanting the juicy gossip on Oscar and the whores!" he laughs.

Oscar drops his fork and scowls directly at him with his eyebrows narrowed in a sharp line, a deadly glare on his face. He sneers back, "For your fucking information, let's be clear. The only whore around here is you and the walking poster boy for STD drugs over there..." Waving his hands at Connor, he continues, "Obviously, when my little hacker nephew here viewed the footage, he didn't realize that it was an escort, not a prostitute that visited the apartment. And to be crystal clear, I touch her, not the other way around!" He goes back to eating once again.

Finn drops back into his chair, seemingly defeated, but he rises once again with a smirk. "Well, bro, nice to know you finally popped your cherry. Let me know the escort agency you use, I'll pass it on to Bren here," he cruelly jokes, slapping Bren on his back before continuing. "Some of us don't have to pay to get our rocks off!" he replies with a cocky smug wink.

Oscar is seething. His eyes darken and he exhales a slow and controlled breath before meeting Finn's eyes with intensity felt all around the table. He smirks back at Finn as he begins to talk. "You're right, perhaps you should use them too, Finn. Then you'd be able to specify the long blonde hair green-eyed innocent girl image that you obviously try to replicate and remind yourself of fucking Angel."

Finn erupts, his chair crashing to the floor as he leaps up and launches himself over the table toward Oscar. Dishes fly and glasses spill.

Luckily Bren is just as quick and starts dragging him back. He plonks Finn in his chair, then rounds his fist and smacks him square on the jaw. "I said, enough!"

Bren casually sits back down in his seat, then continues chewing his food slowly. Oscar is already eating again, Connor lazes back in his chair openly smiling at the drama, Cyn is shaking her head while running back and forth to the kitchen area, I glance at Cal and he rolls his eyes. Clearly this is something that happens regularly. I chance a look at Finn. He looks at me and says, "Welcome to the family, Lily," with a wink. I can't help but bite my lower lip and smile.

CHAPTER 19

Cal

Dinner with my family had gone better than I expected. Reece was obviously agitated, but he'd handled the whole situation well. Da managed to keep his snide remarks to a minimum and no mention was made about the arranged marriage.

After dropping Lily home, I'd taken Reece out for a surprise treat that I'd been arranging for a while. Connor had decided to tag along and I was grateful for his involvement. He was making a clear effort to get to know Reece and that meant a great deal to me.

Reece was blown away when I'd explained we were driving various sports cars around a track for the afternoon. He was even more blown away when I'd told him the LaFerrari Aperta that he'd driven was ours to take home.

Yes, I'd decided to purchase it after hearing how wonderful and amazing Nico Garcia's Ferrari was, and let's face it... I wasn't letting that shithead get the best of me and impressing my son when I had the means and intent to outdo him. So yeah, I thought I'd show them. I purchased the car, knowing full well this was the newest and most expensive model available, one of only 210 ever made. Yeah, Nico Garcia can kiss my ass.

Once we'd arrived home, we had a lazy evening on the couch watching *Fast and Furious*. Lily lay between my legs while I stroked her hair. Reece lay on the floor with the snacks and Puss. We were slowly becoming more open around Reece without realizing it. We were naturally comfortable together and were just relaxing and enjoying each other's company as a family.

Reece had taken himself off to his room, leaving me and Lily alone.

I breathe out a sigh and Lily turns to look at me with concern. "What's wrong?"

I brush my hand through my hair. "Nothing's wrong as such. It's just, I want us to be together properly, I want the world to know you're mine and we're a proper family. I need this shit with Penelope gone."

Lily nods her head in understanding.

"I'm just unsure which way to approach it with her family. The bimbo is quite happy with the arrangement, her father and mine are happy with the arrangement, and unless some fucker backs down, there's going to be major problems because I'm not backing down either."

Lily seems lost in her head for a while, her cute eyebrows knitting together in thought, her focus elsewhere before she asks, "So if Penelope was to back out, where would that leave things? Would she have a say in the arrangement?"

"Baby, she has her fucking father wrapped around her little finger. Problem is, she likes the whole idea of the marriage. She thinks she's got free rein to spend my money and continue living her pompous kept lifestyle and while she thinks that, well then that's the problem."

I exhale with frustration. Why can't the bitch just marry some other sap, a fucking sugar daddy!

Lily narrows her eyes at me. "Cal, seriously you're meant to be clever!" I look at her with confusion.

"You just said, she's happy about it because of what you have to offer. Well, then don't offer it to her."

"Explain..."

"Well, how did she take Reece? Did she realize what a permanent fixture he is in your life? What if you had rules? As her husband, you may have to enforce rules for her to have access to money. Maybe she won't like the rules?" Lily smirks.

I smile to myself while slowly formulating the perfect plan to bring little pompous Penelope Saunders's ideal marriage arrangements crashing down, and with the help of my son, it is going to be fucking epic.

"Lily, you're a fucking genius. I'm going to make Penelope beg not to marry me!" I kiss her nose as we both grin at one another.

CHAPTER 20

Cal

I arrive at Penelope's ridiculously enormous residence with Reece in tow, for a lunch date to move my plan along. This morning started with putting the plan in motion by offering Reece Lucky Charms and sugar-infused pancakes, along with a Gatorade to wash it down.

I pass my key to the valet and knock on the door.

A butler in black and white attire arrives and welcomes us inside the foyer. The house is impressive, I'll give her that, but it just sums up Penelope. Everything is over the top and for show.

The whole entrance is gold-trimmed—gold marble floors, white walls, gold staircase railings, and gold vases on gold pedestals, which give me a flashback to the first time Reece entered my apartment. I smile in memory.

Grinning to myself, I continue with my plan. "Reece buddy, would you look at that vase there? I wonder whose name's underneath?" I nod toward the vase in question.

Of course, the poor kid takes the bait, hook, line, and sinker.

I hear Penelope before I can see her, the *click-clack* of her high heels on the marble floor makes me cringe. She can barely walk in them.

And then there she is, the walking, talking plastic Barbie doll, my fucking fiancée.

A pink minidress barely covers her pussy and her chest heaves out. Surely that's uncomfortable. Her breasts look like they're going to burst with the strain!

As my eyes trail up to her face, I notice her lips are even bigger. How? Fuck, they're enormous. She looks deformed. I quickly avert my gaze before I can stifle a laugh.

A loud *crash* interrupts my evaluation. *Yes, thank you, Reece.* I inwardly grin. I love it when a plan comes together.

"Oh my god! What the hell have you done? You little punk," she snarls, her face reddening, morphing into something resembling a rabid baboon.

Oh no, she did not just call my son that!

"Who the hell do you think you're talking to Penelope?" I erupt with a spiteful tone.

"H..h...he dropped my favorite vase," she screeches.

Reece is standing perfectly still, looking down at the remnants of the vase, unsure if he's going to be in trouble, shifting nervously from foot to foot.

I calm my voice instantly and with one look at my son my temper thaws. "Reece buddy, it's fine, don't worry! In fact, there's another vase over there. Why don't you go and have a look at that one instead?"

He nods and walks over to the next one.

Penelope is seething. I deepen my voice but keep it low. "Penelope, let's get something straight, you do not talk to my son like that, *ever.*"

She flicks her fake-ass long platinum hair over her shoulder in a haughty way. "Whatever." She rolls her eyes and huffs while looking at her nails and feigning boredom. Jesus, it's clear we don't like one another, yet she's prepared to marry me?

Just as I'm about to add to the conversation, in trot two small panting fluffy multicolored dogs. Dressed in fucking tutus. Like literally, the poor things are rainbow-colored, head to fucking toe.

I gasp and shake my head. "Oh Reece, would you look at these poor animals?"

Reece spins around, glaring. "What the fuck happened to them?" he demands, eyes bulging, his feet rocking back and forth on his heels.

"Oh, Toodles and Poodles had a spa day!" she replies, eyes shining with excitement. "They've got a birthday party to go to tomorrow." She's clapping her hands with glee like a child. I cringe at her actions.

I look to Reece and raise an eyebrow. He's shooting daggers at Penelope, who just isn't witnessing the same menacing look and atmosphere as me.

A throat clears behind me. "Shall we proceed to the dining room, ma'am?" the butler asks.

I look toward Reece, whose face is still twisted in a sneer. Clearly, he's also unimpressed. Something tells me Reece isn't going to be able to let the rainbow-colored dogs leave his mind without retribution.

"Reece, why don't you go and explore the property and come and find us in the dining room?" I nod in the direction of the stairs.

He nods before slowly sauntering off, taking in his surroundings with curiosity.

"Erm, excuse me, do you really think your clumsy son

should be walking around unsupervised in my house?" she shrieks.

It pains me to say it. "Tut tut, Penelope, you mean *our* son? As in you're going to be his stepmother soon, therefore he's as good as yours as he is mine, and that's exactly what I'd like to talk to you about."

We sit in the vast dining room, everything is fucking gold. Such a vapid bitch. The butler brings us both a glass of champagne.

"So, as you're soon to be my wife and you'll also be a stepmother to Reece, I have some rules that I require you to abide by."

Her face falls as it dawns on her things may change in her pathetic little life. Her lips quiver. "W..w..what sort of rules?" Her face crumples.

"Well, for starters, you're going to have to earn your allowance and credit card privileges, which will obviously come with a strict limit."

"A limit? Daddy doesn't give me a limit!" she shrieks, mortified.

"Oh, I know, but as part of the agreement we have, my father agreed with your father that it would be me providing for you, and me alone. Therefore, your spending is going to have to be reined in.

"Also, I'm keen for Reece to be homeschooled and I'd like for you to oversee that. Your father reassured mine that you have a stellar education and I'd like you to put that to good use." I casually pop a piece of bread into my mouth, loving her fucking meltdown.

Her face is pure mortification mixed with panic, shock, and despair. "But Daddy paid for me to get good grades, I never actually did the exams," she splutters.

"Oh well, if I'm not satisfied with Reece's progress you

won't be receiving your allowance so you'd better work extra hard." I quickly look away from her and try not to laugh. She's starting to hyperventilate.

"I have needs, Cal. I need money, I need Botox, I need pampering. I cannot and I will not homeschool. What's wrong with his mother?" Her chest reddens.

I sigh dramatically and wave my hand in the air. "Lily? She's perfectly fine but I figured hey, she's had Reece for fourteen years so I might as well take over for the next fourteen, right? Just to clarify, he'll be living with us full-time." I meet her eyes with a pointed look.

"What? You cannot be serious. I cannot live with him. I'm too young to play a mother." Her voice is panicked and even more desperate.

"Oh, you won't be playing mother, you will literally *be the mother*. I know you might find it a little difficult to start, so I've enrolled you in some parenting classes to help you along. You'll be required to attend the Teenagers Autism Are Us group every week too, to give you an insight into what Reece deals with on a daily basis." God, I'm good. She's crumbling before me.

"I will do no such thing. I will tell Daddy. You didn't have a son when we agreed to this." She waves her hand in front of us.

The doors burst open and in walks Reece. I narrow my eyes at him, but he won't look me in the eye. He's up to something. I grin proudly.

"I just went to the restroom," he explains.

I smile to myself. I've been in my son's company long enough now to know he's done something. And for the first time, I do not care. In fact, eat your fucking heart out! I smile to Reece smugly.

He drops down in the chair opposite me. "Would you like a Coke, Reece?"

His eyes shoot up to me in anticipation. "Can I?"

I shrug. "Sure, it's a special occasion after all!"

The butler brings another round of drinks. Penelope drinks her champagne in one mouthful and rudely clicks her fingers. "Bring me another, Jeeves," she snarls, making Reece's eyebrows shoot up and his eyes narrow toward her. She's such a bitch.

"Your butler is called Jeeves?" Reece asks innocently.

"How the hell would I know his name? If I say his name's Jeeves, it's Jeeves. I pay him." She's frantic, red-faced, chest rising and falling as she's still coming to terms with being a stay-at-home stepmom and financially required to follow my rules.

Wow, fucking wow. Reece and I look to one another. Just as I'm about to call her out on that, the butler brings in the food. Reece shifts his gaze toward Penelope's fresh champagne glass.

The butler places a salad down in front of us, but Reece makes a familiar growling noise. "Red shouldn't fucking touch green!" He's tugging his hair and rocking slightly. He picks the tomatoes up and throws them toward Penelope. She should have learned her lesson the first time.

"Penelope, please try and remember when you have Reece in your company, he has certain requirements." I add in a condescending tone, "No red and green touching. Perhaps you'd prefer a book to make notes?" I quirk an eyebrow in her direction.

"I... I...I don't want or need a book. I shouldn't have to deal with this." She throws her arms out toward Reece, spittle flying out of her mouth.

I wave my hand in the air. "Nonsense, you'll get used to

it. You'll be an expert by the time our children come along. In fact, I insist you come off any birth control now so we can put that plan into motion." I look at Reece, who is glaring daggers at me. I wink at him and nod my head. He's brought into my plan as his lips curve into a knowing smirk.

"What the hell are you talking about?" Yep, she's getting louder. Perfect, hysteria—I fucking revel in it.

I exhale dramatically. "Siblings for Reece of course, but you'll be an expert by then so you'll deal with it." I shrug.

She doesn't need to know I'm bullshitting her, but I can't help myself when I'm on a roll.

"Oh, and the fact twins run in the family, yeah you're gonna be fucking huge! Like whale size huge, all stretched and those nasty stretch marks tarnishing that skin of yours. Pity, really." I smile at her. "But no worries. Play your cards right and do as you're told and I'll consider a tummy tuck for you, as a treat, a few years down the line." I inwardly smile.

Penelope drinks her champagne in one go again. Yes, she's losing control. "I need to speak to Daddy. I'm not happy about any of this," she wails, flaying her arms across the table.

"Penelope, calm down. I just want you to fulfill your role as a homemaker. It's no big deal."

"Homemaker? Homemaker? Do I look like a home-maker to you, Cal?" I look her up and down slowly, as if assessing her. I shake my head. "Well not yet, no, but after you've got rid of all the falseness and you've gone back to basics, I'm sure there's something there we can redeem from you and work with," I say while munching nonchalantly on a carrot stick.

A gut-curdling noise comes from Penelope. It's blatantly obvious her stomach is making some serious squelching noises.

"Oh, oh dear." She's clicking her fingers and then picks up a small bell from beside her when she doesn't get an immediate response from the butler. She's ringing the bell for all its worth, shaking it in an alarming way as her stomach grumbles and hisses louder and louder.

"Something's wrong, my stomach is popping, Cal!" She grips her stomach dramatically.

I raise my eyebrows toward her. "Do you need to take a shit, Penelope?" I ask through a tight, amused grin.

She gasps like I've killed her fucking puppy or tutu multicolored dog thing.

"I had a colon cleanse yesterday," she snipes in shock.

Reece scrunches up his nose and avoids my eye. Little fucker has done something, that's for sure.

"Where's Jeeves?" she says in a panicking voice.

"What the fuck's the butler going to do? If you don't go now, you'll shit your panties that's for sure. I might have overdosed you on Visine." Reece shrugs.

"What? What have you done? You've done this to me?" She bawls.

Reece nods his head and smiles proudly, lacing his fingers together on the table in front of him, he leans forward. "Yeah, I told you to leave those poor dogs alone. Anyway... red-eye drops that contain Visine, it was in your bathroom cabinet next to the enema cream. Yeah, Visine causes shits if you swallow it and you've just swallowed a whole lot of it. Hurry to the toilet before you leave that stench permanently on the chair," he says with a cunning smirk.

"Ah, ah, you poisoned me, you poisoned me! Oh god, I've got to go, I've got to go!" She jumps out of her chair, almost breaking her neck with the high heels. Panic running through her, she makes toward the door before turning back. "See yourselves out. I'm talking to Daddy!"

I look at Reece. "Son..." His eyes drop to the table. "That was fucking epic!" I give him my fist for him to bump, his smile is huge as he meets my fist across the table.

As we get up and leave the room, we can hear the *click-clack* of heels and screeching of the bimbo. "Wonder if she made it to the toilet in time?" Reece asks, smirking.

We pass the butler, who is wiping something from the floor, then he moves onto the next spot. I look to Reece, scrunching up my nose at the smell. "Guess not?" I shrug with a gigantic smile.

CHAPTER 21

Lily

Cal was smugly happy with how his dinner went with Penelope. He gave me a debrief and said he was sure he'd hear something from his father soon. I couldn't help but laugh when he told me what had unfolded at Penelope's house. At first, I felt a little sorry for her but after hearing how she spoke to Reece and how conceited she was, my pity soon turned to pride. My boys did good!

Cal had called earlier and Oscar asked if Reece could stay there. They were learning Mandarin together, followed by some war game they were both into. It suited me and Cal just fine and gave us some alone time together.

I'm in my cami top and shorts, lying between Cal's legs. We just watched a movie on the couch. As the end credits begin to roll, I slowly slip farther down between his legs. I turn over and stop when my face comes close to his groin.

He looks gorgeous with his heavy blue eyes filling with lust. His brown wavy hair, a little longer now, has fallen onto his forehead. He cocks a brow at me. I smile and press my mouth to his jeans, licking along his length as the bulge in his jeans grows. Cal's chest rises faster. "Take your top off, Cal. I want to see you." I breathe heavily with need.

He grins, leans forward, and with one hand lifts his white T-shirt off his chest. His gorgeous tanned body leans against the couch cushions. Resting his head back, he looks down at me. I slowly unzip his jeans and pop his top button.

"So, fucking sexy, baby," he breathes.

I lick him through his boxer shorts and his cock twitches beneath my tongue. My eyes remain on Cal's, his heavy with lust.

I gently take the waistband in my hand and pull the boxers down, releasing his heavy throbbing cock.

I start from the bottom and lick to the tip. Cal's breath becomes more ragged. "Fuck baby, take your top off. I need to see your tits."

I ignore him for a moment longer, enjoying the control. I lick his balls and gently suck along the outside of his cock until I get to the top. I lick the bulging head and pull it into my mouth. I lick into his slit, tasting the saltiness on my tongue.

Cal bucks underneath me. When I look up at him, he's biting the side of his mouth with his tense jaw. He's holding back.

"Really need to see those tits, Lily," he says a little deeper this time. I smile at him and sit up. Slowly and purposefully, I lift my top and drag it over my head. My tits bounce as I release my top and Cal grunts. "Fuck."

I push onto my stomach so my head is in his groin, but manage to push my chest onto him so my tits are resting near his balls.

I decide I'd best give him a little show. I know Cal doesn't last long when being tortured but I want this to be about him, not me. I rise slightly. I rub his cock against my tits, around my nipple, one at a time.

"Fuck, I wanna come all over them, baby, all fucking over them. " He licks his lips.

I shake my head innocently. "I want you to come in my mouth, Cal. I need to taste you, is that okay?"

"Fuck, yes, suck my fucking cock, Lily. I ain't gonna last long, baby." His voice is desperate and wanting and my panties dampen with desire.

His breathing intensifies, his moans deepen in his throat as I play with his balls and gently tug them. I work my hand up and down his cock, torturously slow. His hands come up and then back down, as though he doesn't know what to do with them, his fists clenching. It makes me smile to myself, loving how he is losing control.

I suck my mouth over the top of his cock and take him in my mouth, swirling my tongue around his slit, moaning at the saltiness.

I grab his hand and put it to my head, encouraging him to use me.

"Fuck yes, baby," he pants.

He grabs my hair tighter, lifting his hips off the couch as he fucks my mouth, while I continuously move my tongue around him. I can feel my saliva coming out my mouth and it only adds to my wetness pooling between my thighs. Fuck, this is hot!

"Fuck baby, I'm gonna come. Swallow my come, yeah?" His desperate eyes meet mine.

I squeeze his balls as he thrusts into my mouth faster. His come hits my mouth in ropes, falling down my throat as I continue licking him through his thrust. I release him with a pop. Meeting his eyes, I pull his weakening cock back to my mouth and lick him clean, making sure he's watching every movement my tongue makes.

He pants as his breathing slows. "Fuck, baby that was intense."

I gently release him from my mouth and smile at him. "Mmm, very tasty, Mr. O'Connell." I smirk, flirtatiously.

Cal looks at me deeply, sending shivers up my spine. "I'm taking you both away tomorrow. I've arranged a surprise. You should probably go shower and wait for me on our bed naked. I've got a few phone calls to make and then I'll join you." He slowly pushes my hair behind my ear in a sweet gesture.

I move off him and just as I am about to walk away, Cal catches my wrist in his hand. "I fucking love you. You know that, right?"

I smile back to him. "Of course!"

Wow, that was a little weird.

CAL

I've just gotten off the phone with my livid father, who's just spat venom down the phone line to me. I've been told what a fucking useless waste of space I am, a little selfish prick, complete incompetent fucker, waste of air, and deserved to have my balls cut off, blah blah blah. I let him rant while I sat back on the couch and smiled to myself, quite pleased with the turn of events.

Poor Mr. Saunders called him this evening and insisted he'd been duped into the business arrangements and called for them to be obsolete, mainly due to the fact the marriage was not going ahead. Penelope had told him my expectations in the marriage had traumatized her. Mr. Saunders had also rightly pointed out that information about me was not available to him before he made the agreement, referring to Reece and my commitments as a father and Reece being my future successor, not the impending baby they'd concocted in their deranged heads.

Of course, my father was seething. I rolled my eyes at the whole never-fucking-step-foot-in-this-house-again bullshit he was spewing. I only wish I didn't have to and he'd follow through with that one.

After him telling me to "fuck right off, you selfish little fucking bastard, you're no son of mine," he ended the call. I was over the fucking moon. I was finally free, free to make my own choices, and finally free to make my family my own and official.

I walk into our bedroom. unable to hold back the smile I'm wearing.

Opening the door to find Lily completely naked, as asked, is the icing on the fucking cake. My cock instantly rising in my pants, I release a groan.

"You have no idea how fucking gorgeous you look right now, baby." My eyes eat up her beautiful as fuck body.

She looks at me with a raised eyebrow and a smirk on her beautiful face. She has no idea how fucking gorgeous she is. Her hair splayed out over the pillows, her green eyes taunting me with a promise of pleasure, she's the most beautiful sexy woman I've ever seen.

Her legs are open and her delicious pussy bared to me. A small trimmed trail of curls surrounds her clit and my mouth waters at the sight. I pull my eyes up to her tits, her perfect fucking tits sitting there waiting for me to mark, waiting for me to lick and coat with my come. Her nipples sharpen under my gaze. I lick my lips.

A small chuckle escapes Lily's mouth, a teasing grin on her face. My eyes flash to hers in question.

I approach the bed, pulling down my jeans and boxers in one go. Freeing my cock, I fist it roughly. Trailing a line down her pussy with my finger I tell her, "So fucking gorgeous. I'm going to eat this juicy little pussy, then I'm going to fuck you and make you come on my cock. How does that sound, beautiful?"

Lily moans in response. A small smirk graces my lips. Yeah, she wants this as bad as me.

I crawl over Lily and stop at her thighs, opening them wider. I hold her open for me while peppering kisses around her legs. Slowly I lick her slit from bottom to top. I look up to her to see she's watching me with her bottom lip pulled between her teeth. She looks me in the eyes and moves her hand to her tits and begins to rub them. Fuck that's hot. I moan into her pussy. I'm so fucking hard and so fucking aroused I start grinding my cock into the fucking mattress like a horny teenager. "You taste like temptation, needy, greedy, mine!" I pant each word out between a lick from top to bottom, from bottom to top, her arousal coating my tongue.

Lily fists the sheets, tightening them in her hands. She starts to fuck my face as I latch onto her clit, sucking and licking her faster and faster. I rub my nose into her greedy clit as I thrust my tongue into her pussy hole. Her breathing is becoming ragged and the sounds leaving her mouth are fucking hot.

"Ah, fuck, Cal. Like that!" Moan after moan leaves her mouth as her hips jerk harder against my face, her hips rising off the bed.

I put two fingers together and thrust them into her sopping wet pussy. I push deep and bend my fingers to curve inwards, hitting the spot. She stills with the impact, completely releases her orgasm as her body shakes, and she lets out a loud groaning scream. So, fucking hot.

I crawl up her body and grab her chin between my fingers, roughly. I force my tongue into her mouth as she kisses me back with animalistic passion, our tongues tangled together. She tastes herself on me. Pulling my head toward hers, her tongue wraps around mine. She's trying to regain control over me. Fuck that.

I stop kissing her and grab her wrists. I pin them above her head as I thrust into her, ramming her on my cock. She releases a loud "ah"—a moan of satisfaction, her eyes desperate with desire and need.

I pump into Lily while holding her wrists above her head and sucking on her left nipple, swirling the tip around my tongue with vigor. Feeling the bounce of her tit against my face is sending me into overdrive, my balls tingle and I clamp my teeth down on Lily's tit to try and ward off the impending orgasm.

I suckle her breast into my mouth, groaning, loving the soft smooth skin touching my tongue. I could play with these fuckers all day. Fuck, what were they like when she was pregnant? Pregnant with our son. I glance down to her stomach—her flat toned stomach. A sudden need to fill her with my baby overwhelms me. The thoughts of Lily pregnant nearly makes me lose my load.

My orgasm is fast approaching.

"Cal, I'm going to come again."

Thank fuck, I can release myself!

I release her nipple with a pop and bite down on her tit again, although not hard enough to break the skin.

Her pussy clenches around me as I drive into her harder and faster until "ffffuuuuckkk," I scream my release. Lily throws her head back and her pussy spasms around my cock. It's so fucking tight and intense, the pulses of her pussy ripple through me as she milks my cock. "Fuck," I chant again, looking down on my cock still inside her. I hope my come has knocked her up.

We both slowly come down from our orgasms. Panting, I roll onto my back. I pull Lily with me so she's in the crook of my neck. She throws her leg over my waist and we lie there together, completely and utterly spent.

I gently draw circles around the skin on her arm. I listen for her breathing to see if she has fallen asleep.

"Are you awake?"

Lily giggles. "Only just. You nearly knocked me out with orgasms!"

I laugh back, but feel a little nervous about my next topic of conversation. I lick my lips with apprehension. "Have you considered when you'd like to start trying for a baby? I mean, we aren't getting any younger, Lily."

Lily stills beside me, her body becoming stiff. "I don't want any more children, Cal."

My heart races. What the fuck? My words probably come out harsher than they should. "What the fuck do you mean, you don't want any more children?"

Lily turns her head to face me. "I can't go through having any more children. I'm sorry, it's not something I'm prepared to do and if that's what you want? Perhaps you need to reconsider things between us before they get even more serious."

My heart is pounding out of my chest. Is she for fucking real right now? Reconsider?

"So, you were prepared to have Nico Garcia's fucking kid but you can't have mine. Is that what you're saying?" I snipe.

Lily shoots up, the sheets pooling around her tits, her nipples and my marks on full display, making it difficult for me to have an argument with her right now. "Are you for real right now, Cal? I lost a fucking baby, I brought our son up alone, I did every fucking thing alone! I won't go through any of that again, Cal. Ever!"

My heart sinks. I hear the words she's saying but I won't accept them. I wait a few moments and collect my words because I need her to understand. I breathe slowly and turn my tone gentle. "I never had any of that, Lily. I never got to see your stomach grow. Hell, I don't even know what my own son looked like as a baby or small child. I never heard his first words, nothing. I want to be there, for you and Reece and our fucking baby. I want to experience it all. Can you please consider that before you completely give up on the baby subject?" She can't give up on that idea, it's all I ever wanted—her and a family. I won't let her give up on it. It's not a fucking option. My jaw clenches in frustration.

Lily takes a deep breath and puts her head down on me, her breathing tickling the hairs on my chest. "It's early days for us, Cal. Please don't push me for things I never considered. Let's just take one day at a time, get to love the family we have already, and take it from there."

I stroke her head in a soothing way. I'm sure she takes this as me agreeing to her thoughts, but fuck that. I've waited my entire life for a family with her and this baby is going to happen. I'm going to make sure I experience all the things I should have done with Reece. She'll soon come around and realize I'm here to stay and support her and our growing family.

I smile to myself as a small plan is starting to take hold in my head.

CHAPTER 22

Lily

Cal woke me early this morning with a suitcase packed and Reece ready and waiting to go on a surprise trip. Reece wasn't as anxious as I'd expect him to be, so I wondered if Cal had spoken to him to give him a heads up.

We drove for just over two hours to a beautiful hotel near Cape May. It had a cluster of villas with access directly onto a private beach. Cal checked us in and then drove to our villa. It was small but airy at the same time. There was a small kitchenette at the front followed by an open-plan concept with dining area and lounge. Floor to cciling bi-folding doors led outside onto a small patio with a dining table and sun loungers, then straight to the beach and ocean. The sand was white and the sea was shining under the sun. Cal explained that a bedroom led off each side of the kitchen and cach had its own bathroom. Reece went straight to a bedroom to change into his swimwear.

"He's eager to go in the sea, apparently," Cal says on a chuckle.

I laugh. "Yeah, you might actually be surprised. His whole demeanor changes when we go to the beach. He just seems to relax more."

Cal looks at me. "Really?"

I shrug. "Yeah, he loves to lay on the sun loungers and actually falls asleep. The whole atmosphere relaxes him."

"I'll go drag the sun loungers closer to the water. The fridge is fully stocked. You go get changed, I'll pack us up, and I'll meet you outside, baby."

Cal leans in and kisses me. My heart warms and I can't help but tug him closer to me and deepen the kiss. My hands curl into his hair behind his neck as I pull him closer. His hands squeeze my ass and I clench my thighs together with need.

Cal moves his head to the side to spy for Reece coming back. We hear movement at the door and Cal breaks the kiss quickly. "Fuck," he says as he rearranges his bulge, pulling his T-shirt over his shorts.

My face is heated and my panties are wet. I could so climb him right now! I bite my lip.

"You need sunscreen on, Mom. Your face is red already," Reece says as he waltzes past me out the doors to the beach.

Cal chuckles nervously, running his hand through his waves. "That was fucking close, Lily. You're naughty, you know that?" He smacks my ass as he walks past, following Reece outside.

CAL

Today is turning out to be one of the best days of my life. Lily looks fucking edible in her tight green bikini. Her fucking ass cheeks half hang out as she walks, making it difficult for me not to bend her over and fuck her then and there.

Reece is like a different kid here. He's truly relaxed. We've played in the sea and Reece insisted we throw a ball to one another for well over an hour. Not bad for a kid that hates sports.

Lily's gone to fetch burgers for us from the hotel restaurant so now is my chance to speak to Reece. He's been on his tablet awhile, relaxing on the lounger in the shade.

I clear my throat. "So the deal is off with Penelope now, Reece..."

He looks at me expectantly.

"So basically, I'm free to do whatever I want now." I shift nervously as I try to gauge a reaction from him. I'm hoping he can read me but I'm not sure that I'm making it clear enough.

"What I really want, Reece, is to make you and your mom my family, officially I mean..."

Reece is still looking at me, not a single sign or reaction on his face telling me he understands. Fuck, this is hard work. I brush my hand through my hair and drag my hand down my face in frustration.

My voice is low and I tug on my hair. "I really want to marry your mom, Reece. What do you think?" I look at him nervously.

Reece shifts, sitting up to fully face me. He glares at me with a serious look on his face, eyebrows narrowed. "I think you should have grown some balls and told your fucking dad you weren't marrying that bitch!" he venomously spits out. I almost choke. I look at him with my mouth gaping open, not sure what to say.

"I'm pleased you finally grew some balls and did something about it. I was starting to think I'd have to take matters into my own hands. I was surveying the place when we visited her, you know scoping it out..." He wafts his hands around nonchalantly, sounding like some sort of little fucking gangster. Jesus, we've got our work cut out.

"Anyway, seemed like the bitch couldn't handle us, hey?" He puts his fist out for me to bump and I slowly move my fist toward his, not sure what I'm bumping fists for.

Is this confirmation that he's okay with me marrying his mom?

"I won't be your best man though, cos Mom's gonna want me to walk her down the aisle. You know that, right?"

Guess I had my answer right there. I smile. "No problem, buddy. I understand."

He nods and lies back down, resting his head against the cushion. He looks deep in thought. I sit a little while longer, watching him, almost frozen. I want to know what he is thinking but don't want to crowd him at the same time. I sit back on the lounger and slowly relax.

A few minutes pass by when Reece sharply turns his head toward me, his face all serious and I immediately feel defensive.

"Dad?" Wow, that's the first time Reece has called me Dad. My heart flips and I feel an immediate emotion of pride and shock. I turn to face him, looking into his eyes, the same eyes as mine, our emotions mirrored.

"Can I tell you something? But you're not allowed to tell anyone, okay?"

I nod. "Sure, you can tell me anything, Reece." I swallow my emotions thickly.

He stares at me, eyes swimming with emotion. He gulps. "When Pussy was a kitten, she went outside and disappeared all day. I was freaking out and Mom couldn't find her. Puss came back inside later and she brought a fucking blackbird with her. It was dead." He looks perplexed and I wonder where the fuck he is going with this, if anywhere at all.

"Anyway, I was so upset and freaked out because I liked little fucking birds and she just destroyed one. Mom put a bell on her and said it was a warning bell, so no other blackbirds could ever be taken. I told Mom she was going to be an indoor cat, but we left the bell on her just in case." He nods his head to his own story and I look at him, unsure what to say.

Reece gulps again. "I remembered Greg spoke to us about warning each other in secret, like in a code, and I thought it was a good idea to use a word nobody else would understand but me and my mom. So we agreed that if there was an emergency or we needed to follow a certain procedure we would use the word 'blackbird,' you know, like a bit of an SOS?"

I nod, understanding what he was telling me. "That night when you came to our apartment, I texted Mom 'Blackbird.' She knew what she had to do."

I look at him, a little choked up that'd he'd shared a secret with me. He was trusting me. "That's amazing Reece, I'm really proud of you for coming up with that and thank you for sharing it. It means a lot to me, buddy. Thank you."

Reece holds his head down as he toes the sand around his feet. "Well, you can use it too, right? If ever we need one another, we text 'blackbird,' okay?"

"Yeah, that's brilliant." I beam at him, take a quick drink of my water, and a deep breath for courage. "Reece, I love you man."

His head shoots up and he laughs. "Of course you do. Who fucking wouldn't, right?"

I laugh, really fucking laugh, and Reece joins me.

LILY

It's been a truly memorable day for us all. Cal has been in his element, enjoying playing the dad role. Reece has even started calling him Dad, and the pride in Cal's smile is to die for. I couldn't be happier.

Cal and I have decided to take a walk along the shoreline as the sun sets, leaving Reece in the villa. Apparently, Reece had more important things to do. Cal had scoffed when Reece threw himself on the couch with his tablet. He'd wanted him to come with us.

To be honest, I was enjoying the alone time with Cal. We hadn't had much of it and over the years it's been very difficult to find any time away from Reece at all.

We're walking hand in hand, barefoot with our feet at the shoreline. Cal seems a little off. He isn't talking much and I wonder if it was because Reece hadn't joined us.

Or was the baby conversation playing on his mind?

"You okay?"

He stops walking, turns toward me, giving me a small smile that looks almost fake. My stomach plummets.

"What's the matter, Cal? Did something happen?"

He puts his hand through his hair and tugs it. "Actually, I have something to ask you."

"Oh, okay." I nibble my finger, wondering what the hell is wrong. Has Reece done something?

Cal slowly gets down on one knee at the water's edge. Opening a black box, he holds it out to me—a small delicate white-gold band with a square diamond in the center. It's understated and totally me, not flashy in any sense.

"Lily, from the first moment in Vegas, I knew you were the one for me. I was young, stupid, so fucking hesitant." He shakes his head, remembering our time together. "That one night with you was what I called the best night of my fucking life. We created another life and I wish with all my heart I could go back and be the man I wanted to be that night, the one who returned to your room and spent the rest of my life dedicated to you and our baby."

Cal's eyes are cast down. I know he feels strongly about our past. We both have regrets and I know it eats him up inside that he's missed Reece's childhood years.

"I wasted years regretting what could have been, what should have been. I'm not prepared to waste another moment. You and Reece are my everything. I'll never be anything other than the man and father you both deserve. I'm going to spend the rest of my life making it up to you both. I love you more than you can ever imagine, Lily. Will you do me the honor of being my wife, forever and always?"

My heart is beating hard through my chest. He's the most handsome, strong, and supportive man I've ever come across. I choke out my words through tears, swallowing thickly, I tell him, "I love you, Cal, more than ever. Of course I will. Come here!"

He picks me up around the waist and I wrap my legs

around him. He kisses me deeply. I groan into his mouth as our tongues lash together.

"Fuck, I need you!" Cal gasps.

I rub myself against his erect cock, through his shorts. My dress rides up around my waist as his hands squeeze my ass cheeks.

I smile into the kiss. Thank god we're out of sight of the villa and nobody can see us here.

Cal turns us and starts walking farther into the water. "Cal, what the hell are you doing?" I screech in panic. Is he insane?

He chuckles. "Do you know how fucking tempting you've been in that skimpy goddamn bikini? Tormenting me, tormenting my cock? I've had to hide my fucking hard-on most of the day. I've been unable to relieve myself and adjust myself properly because our teenage son is constantly around us. So, my fiancée..." We're now waist-deep in the water and I'm clinging on to Cal for dear life, my arms hanging around his neck. "Now I'm going to fuck you in the sea like I've been wanting to do all fucking day!"

I kiss him, my tongue plummeting into his mouth. His hands are on my ass, but in a frantic scramble, he tugs my panties to the side as my hand pulls his throbbing cock free from his shorts. I guide him to my entrance as I sink onto him. He pushes me down with force, not giving me time to adjust as he thrusts in and out of me, causing me to pant and moan into his mouth.

"Fuck, Cal, that's incredible. Fuck me hard!"

He smirks into our kiss as he continues the assault on me. My orgasm builds as I wrap my legs tighter around him, rubbing myself up and down as he thrusts in and out. My clit is rubbing against his pubic bone and my pussy is clenching around him as the orgasm begins to take control.

Cal's breathing becomes more erratic as he seems determined to push through my orgasm. My pussy clenching his
cock tighter, he groans and grips my ass with such force I
know I'm going to be bruised.

"Ah fuck...ah fuck," he chants through the bruising kiss.

"Yes, Cal. Yes." My hands dig into his neck, my nails
bloodying his skin as he fucks me hard through my orgasm.
I feel his cock throb as he releases his come into me, making
me shudder. Slowly our kiss becomes more loving and
longing as our breathing slowly becomes more controlled.

"Love you, baby."

"Love you, Cal."

He pecks my lips again and again. I close my eyes and we
rest our foreheads against one another, both completely
satiated.

CHAPTER 23

Lily

It's been a couple of weeks since Cal proposed and we've created a nice routine in pre-wedded bliss.

However, today is Thursday and Cal has been miserable all morning due to the fact he's got to fly out to Boston for a few meetings with Bren and Oscar. He's going to be gone until Saturday and he hates that he has to leave us.

He's even tried convincing me to withdraw Reece from school for the two days, but Reece has won two awards at school and the presentation is this afternoon. That's another reason Cal isn't happy   he's missing out on another memorable event in Reece's life.

I feel bad for him. I said I'd record it for him and FaceTime him as soon as we get out of the presentation so he can speak to me and Reece but ultimately there isn't much more we can do about it.

Cal is the second son in the family and he's expected to work alongside Bren, making deals and dealing with the business associates. So he needs to be there whether he likes it or not.

He'd reluctantly left us this morning like a pouting child. He peppered me with kisses and mumbles of "I love you" and "missing you already." He was unbelievably sweet and I love this side of him. Reece had barely mumbled a goodbye to Cal, which pissed him off all the more. I'd rolled my eyes at Cal's doe-eyed expression and shrugged at him. I was used to the lack of affection from Reece, but Cal longed for it.

CAL

I'd been a moody ass all fucking day. The weather was shit, the meetings went shit, and my mood was shit.

We were now being driven back to the hotel and finally Lily FaceTimed me. My mood changes in an instant and I perk up with the biggest smile on my face. "Hey baby," I coo like a pussy.

"Hey, Cal, guess what?" Her bright green eyes shine with pride.

"Go on..." I prompt with a grin. She knows I don't like to be kept waiting.

"So, our son won two awards. One for Best Coder in Information Technology.'"

I chuckle. "Obviously he did!"

Both Bren and Oscar laugh in the car, both listening in with smiles of their own.

Reece chimes in, "Yeah, beat that fucker, Boris, Dad!"

I laugh. "That's my boy!" I'm beaming with pride.

"And..." Lily continues "...you'd never guess what his other award is for." She's loving dragging this out, the little minx.

"Go on baby, shock me!" I tease back.

"He only went and won an award for Showing Compassion and Support to Another," Lily declares, suddenly teary-eyed.

Wow. That was a big fucking deal, more so than the IT award. We know Reece is more than capable in the technology department but, support and compassion? This just proved how far Reece has come and how much his interpersonal skills were improving.

Yeah, proud fucking dad here!

I choke up a little, then look around the car. Both Bren and Oscar are looking at me, small smiles gracing their faces. Bren nods in a silent acknowledgment of how far we've come, while Oscar gives a brief cocky smirk in a knew-he-could-do-it way.

I feel so damn lucky, lucky to share this with my brothers, and lucky to have Lily and Reece.

I clear my throat. "Fuck baby, that's amazing." She can hear my pride and emotion in my voice.

"It is, isn't it?" She beams.

"Sure is. I'm so proud of you, Reece," I shout louder. Lily turns the phone to Reece, who is walking off in front with his AirPods in, not a care in the world, and completely oblivious to his parents having a proud emotional moment about him.

"Are you heading home now?"

"Yeah, we're just getting to the cars. Are two security cars really necessary?" she scolds.

I grin to myself, "Just keeping you both safe in my absence."

"Mmm," she rolls her eyes at me.

"You gonna call me tonight, right?"

She lets out a puff of air and chuckles. "Yes, Cal, I'll call you tonight and let you know we're all tucked up in bed."

"Good girl. Speak to you later. Love you!"

She smiles broadly. "Love you."

She ends the call and I relax back into my seat with a satisfied smile on my face.

Bren laughs. "Fuck man, you are well and truly fucking pussy-whipped!"

"Yeah, I am, aren't I?" And I was so fucking happy about it too.

LILY

Reece is lost in his head as we pull away from the school. I tuck my purse down on the floor and settle into the drive home.

We're about ten minutes into the drive on a country lane when everything happens so fast and instantaneously, I don't have time to think or react.

An almighty explosion from behind us causes our car to careen with the impact. Our driver glances in his rearview mirror and then glances back toward me. "Shit," is the only response he gives. I know instantly it's the SUV that follows behind us.

Out of the corner of my eye, I see a black SUV pull out of the side road. It hits us so quickly I don't even register what's happening. I feel nothing, just emptiness and blackness. The only thing I see through blurry vision is Reece grabbing his phone from his backpack. I don't even know if he managed to do anything with it. Darkness smothers me as I gasp for air.

CHAPTER 24

Lily

I can hear voices, but I can't pinpoint where they are or who they belong to.

My head throbs, my right leg is painful but numb. My wrists hurt. My legs aren't moving. What the hell is happening to me? My head pounds with an unusual intensity.

There's a strange damp smell and a constant dripping noise. It occurs to me that I'm not in a hospital. I'm injured and hurt but not in a hospital. Where the hell am I?

I force my eyes open, but the movement makes my head hurt. I wince at the pain. Unsure of what's hurt me, I try to move my legs again but then I realize they aren't moving because they're tied down. What the hell? I look at my legs, they're tied down to a metal chair.

I look at my hands, they're tied in front of me and I have a fucking knife sticking out of my right thigh. What the hell is happening? I begin to panic, gasping, my chest rising and falling swiftly.

"Ah, nice of you to join us, Abi!" His voice is full of disdain as he spits the words out at me. My heart sinks.

I slowly take in the man in front of me. Nico sits wide-legged in gray fitted pants, brown shoes, and a white shirt with his top buttons open. His olive skin is on full display. His face is still sharp, with a five o'clock shadow. He looks as handsome as ever, but his eyes? They're as cold and as black as the day I lost the baby. There's no warmth left in them. They drill into me with such displeasure I have to avert my gaze.

I flick my focus around the room, becoming acutely aware that I'm in some sort of warehouse. A metal roof covers us, open pipework releases a drizzle of water onto the cement floor.

To Nico's right is the man whose sole purpose has been to destroy my character and help fuel his hatred of me, Raul Garcia Senior. I close my eyes, willing them to disappear. This can't be happening.

Yes, I am well and truly in the shit!

"Wh...what am I doing here, Nico? Where's Reece?"

"Ah, you mean Jacob, yes? Or are there other names you call yourselves when you run like thieves in the night, hmmm?" He rubs his finger absently along his jawline and I look back up to him.

He's so calm, collected, and eerily in control, nothing like the loveable Nico I once adored. His hair is longer now and slicked back, much like his older brothers. I can't help but think how much they are alike now—handsome, cold, cruel, merciless, and heartless. This is not the Nico I knew.

The words speed out of my mouth in panic. "You made a mistake, Nico. You never gave me a chance to explain, none of it was what you thought, I swear it!" Can he not hear the truth and desperation in my voice?

He raises an eyebrow, but it isn't in question. No, it's a mocking gesture.

"I made a mistake, Abigail? Really? I made a mistake?" His voice is deep, sneering, and aggressive as he thumps his fist against his chest.

Movement catches my eye as Raul shuffles gleefully on his chair. "Cut the crap, Nico, get the information from her and have done with her," he snaps, seemingly annoyed at our exchange. He glances at his watch. "We have things to do," he prompts.

I start to panic. I've not seen or heard Reece and things are being pushed along. My time is running out and judging by the knife in my leg, they are prepared to take things to the next level.

"Where are our shipments, Abigail?" Nico leans forward into my face. "Do you need a little prompting?" he mocks, his eyes divert to something or someone behind me and he nods. I try turning to look. A door behind opens, followed by two sets of footsteps. I close my eyes, not wanting to see for sure because I know in my heart one of them is Reece. Panic starts to rise in my chest, sheer terror. What are they going to do?

My eyes shoot open at the silence. Nico holds his hand up and the guard beside Reece stops in his tracks. Nico gestures for Reece to step forward.

Reece is now in my line of sight. He looks okay. He vaguely looks my way but then concentrates on Nico. He's so controlled I'm not sure where he's getting the confidence from.

CHAPTER 25

Cal

W e're five minutes out from the hotel when my phone vibrates with a text. I see Reece's name and smile to myself. It's short-lived when I see the one word that causes my emotions to come crumbling down around me...*blackbird*.

My face must have morphed into something of sheer panic because Oscar is quick to respond without hesitation or question. He tries calling Lily's driver, Angelo, to no avail.

"What's wrong?" Bren barks.

I can't breathe, I can't explain, I feel as though I'm having a panic attack.

Oscar takes over. "Cal's just received a text and I think it's to say something's wrong. Am I right?" he asks. All I can do is nod, my mind hazy with panic, my head filled with an unfamiliar fog.

"What the fuck's wrong? With who? Cal, fucking speak man!" Bren barks.

I shake my head and pull my hair, my voice quivering.

"It's Reece. He's sent me an SOS text, it was a code text for when he needs help. Something's happened, something's happening, I don't know! What the fuck do I do?" I ask, pleading with panic and desperation, meeting Bren's eyes.

"It's okay man, we got this!" His hand rests on my shoulder as he gestures toward Oscar.

Oscar is already tapping away on his tablet. "Driver, airport NOW!" he roars. It's rare for Oscar to raise his voice but I'm past caring. I need to know where they are and what's happening.

"Cal, pull yourself together. Inform Connor and Finn. Let them lead things in New Jersey. Oscar, you track them down. I'll pull a security team together and they'll be at our disposal as soon as Oscar has a lead."

I nod my head as we get to work.

We board the plane back to New Jersey. As soon as we are seated, Oscar settles down to work. I'm about to open my mouth when he puts his finger up to stop me. He's working furiously, tapping away on his tablet.

Bren walks over to the table we're sitting at and opens a laptop. Oscar links the tablet and laptop. I look to him for an explanation.

"They've obviously destroyed their phones, but I've managed to track them via Reece's watch. Reece also managed to turn his app on, the one on his watch. It's saved me some time to hack into it. I'm just hacking their systems now. We should be able to use any cameras in their area. Hopefully, they're somewhere with cameras in the room." I breathe out in relief. Thank fuck Reece has managed to save us some time.

We sit in silence as Oscar types away frantically.

"Here." He points to the screen.

On the screen is a warehouse. It looks empty apart from....

Lily strapped to a metal fucking chair. She's opposite some dickhead I don't recognize and at the side, fucking Raul Garcia Senior. So is the other guy Nico?

I hope to fuck it is because then there's a small chance he may still have feelings and compassion for Lily and Reece. Greg said as much, right?

God, my stomach roils. I could throw up. My legs bounce with nerves. Bren's still barking orders into the phone, demanding my brothers' teams search warehouses until we know more.

Oscar zooms in closer. I sit, eyes glued to the screen, as Reece is brought through a door behind Lily. I close my eyes to prepare myself and open them with bated breath. Oscar turns the volume up.

"Jacob, you've grown!" Nico coos.

Reece smiles. "Yeah, I'm fourteen now, Nicky," he replies proudly. Nicky? He calls the douche Nicky?

Nico smiles but it's a small and solemn smile. I assume it's to do with the nickname.

My heart thumps harder. Please still fucking care for them.

Reece stands taller. "Nico, I need to confess something to you and you're gonna be cross but you need to hear me out, okay?" Reece fidgets with his hands.

Lily's panicked and desperate voice vibrates off the walls, causing her veins to throb at the side of her neck. She's red-faced and distraught, her desperate pleas go ignored. "Reece no, please don't do this! Redcars, Reece, do you hear me?"

Reece shakes his head, blocking out Lily's pleas.

"No, it's okay, Mom. I'm going to explain to Nico what happened and everything will be okay." Reece is nodding to himself confidently as if he's convincing himself what he's about to do is the right thing.

Nico straightens in his chair, eyebrow raised. "Go on, Jacob, fill me in."

"Everything that happened, Nico, was my fault, all of it. But I didn't mean it. I swear I didn't mean it."

Lily's sobs are muffling her pleas.

Nico looks to Lily and back at Reece, confused.

"Cut the bullshit, kid. Nico, fucking shoot the kid or something. Get her to talk." Raul Garcia spits his venom, growing increasingly impatient. The atmosphere is at a boiling point, we can feel the tension from here.

Nico stretches out his legs calmly and turns his glare up to Reece, who is beginning to pull on his hair, showing the pressure of the situation.

My heart is pounding through my chest. I can't stop my eyes watering as I'm hopelessly watching the scene unfold in front of me, my body shaking. I need to get the fuck home. I need my family safe. My eyes desperately search Oscar's for answers to their location. He shakes his head.

"When my mom told you that your papa had been mean to her and called her names, you didn't listen, Nico. You never fucking listened. You let him treat her like shit, Nico." Reece is riled up, his face red with emotional pain and tears. The scene is difficult to watch. My son's tugging at his hair in frustration, his voice quivering.

Raul starts to laugh, mocking. He stabs his finger into his chest for emphasis. "Treat her like shit? My son, my heirs, should marry an untouched woman, not a woman outside of our own, with a child already! What you're spouting is nothing my son doesn't already know, nothing we haven't already discussed.

"Now keep to the subject and tell us *where the fuck* is our cargo!" he booms, his face growing redder, spit flying from his mouth with each angry word.

My insides churn. Raul fucking Garcia is a loose cannon and Reece is well and truly pissing him off. My fists are clenching in my hand, making my knuckles turn white. *Please, Reece, lay the fuck off*, I chant in my head. The situation is getting out of control.

Nico is growing visibly agitated at his father's outburst. It's clear he seems somewhat defensive of Reece.

"Jacob, your mom stole from me, my family. You're old enough now to know that what she did has consequences. We need our cargo back, Jacob, and one way or another I intend to get it."

Lily is sobbing, she's a mess. "Please, Nico, you don't understand!"

"*Stop!*" Reece screams. He's pulling his hair, his body shaking. "*Stop*, Nico, you're not listening, you never fucking listened. It wasn't my mom who took your cargo, it was me!"

Raul starts to laugh, fucking belly laughs, at Reece's outburst. Nico's eyes narrow and look at Reece. He sees some truth in Reece's words because his face grows softer and curious.

"I heard them talking about my mom. Mr. Garcia and your brother Raul, they said, 'Tenemos que deshacernos de la zorra y su hijo.' We need to get rid of the bitch and her son." Reece exhales and continues, "she tried to tell him I hit her; he didn't believe her."

"My mom told you, Nico, that your papa hit her, that he called her a whore and a bitch. She told you and you did nothing. You said she was making things difficult and you never listened.

"I heard them. Me! They said they could do anything and you'd believe them, not my mom."

Reece is getting out of breath and shaking. "Your papa said Raul could have her and fuck her as he likes. That's my mom, Nico! You should have listened. They were going to hurt her! And you wouldn't listen."

Nico stands abruptly and spins to face Raul. "What's he talking about?" he demands, his words seething from his mouth.

"The kid's a fucking little liar like his mama. Now, you either put a bullet in the kid and get me my cargo shipment or I'll do it myself."

Nico raises his hand to halt his father's movements. His words are calm and collected. "I said, what the fuck is he talking about? You hit her?" Disgust oozes from Nico's stern voice.

"I was keeping your bitch in line. Clearly you're not man enough to sort the little whore out yourself."

Nico's spine straightens. His body bolts sharply, almost like electricity has powered through him, an awareness settling inside him. His glare is razor-focused on his father.

"Nico," Reece sniffles. "I'm sorry I caused the trouble. I didn't realize how serious it all was. I just wanted him to pay for hurting my mom. I was good on the computers you brought me, Nico, real fucking good. And I learned your language. I wanted to impress you, but then I heard things and didn't want everyone to know that I knew what you were all saying." Reece shakes his head, remembering.

"I heard about the shipments. I heard how fucking excited Mr. Garcia was that everything was going to plan. I was dumb. I thought, fuck it, I'm going to hurt him. I thought it would be funny. I know now I'm older, *how fucking stupid* I was!" Reece spits the words out, frustrated with himself, tugging his hair and groaning. "So fucking stupid, I was, Nico." He shakes his head.

Nico stands as still as a statue, completely dumb-founded. "You took the shipment?" His voice is void of any emotion.

Lily frantically tugs at her wrists, trying to free herself.

Reece steps forward again. "I did, Nico. I can give them back, I swear!" He closes his eyes and takes a deep breath. "Cargo shipment order 122047, San Juan Westbound to Tijuana via Ensenada, crate reference 0192-126. Red writing, with a GD logo on the side." He nods to himself as if giving confirmation that he's got the shipment details correct.

Nico looks down at his feet, his hands on his hips, and then looks back toward Reece, his face stunned.

"Nico, you hear this? You let these scumbags into our house? Our compound, you let them manipulate you, Nico," his father protests, mockingly.

Oscar is as transfixed by the screen as me. Bren is off in the background barking at someone on the phone, but it's all background noise to me as I watch, completely unsure how this is all going to pan out for my family. I'm completely and utterly helpless.

"You hit her, Papa? Threatened her with rape? Call her a slut? Mmm? You did those things Jacob is saying? Answer me goddamn it!" Nico screams at his father.

His father looks smug, unfazed by Nico's outburst. Nico pulls a gun from his back and points it toward Reece.

My body stops working, my legs would give way if I wasn't already sitting down.

"Nico, Nico, please. I'm begging you please, that's my baby. Please, Nico, I've lost one baby, please don't let me lose another. Please!" Lily is completely distraught. Nico turns his head toward her and his face softens from the steel exterior he's previously portraying. His eyes lock with Lily as he gives her a soft sympathetic smile followed by a small nod as he turns back toward his father and Reece.

Nico's finger hits the trigger of the gun pointed in Reece's direction, but Reece doesn't fall to the floor. It's the guard standing beside Reece that drops. Lily's scream echoes around the room.

Nico's father jumps out of his chair and no sooner has he taken a step toward Nico, Nico pulls the trigger again. Instantly, Raul Garcia Senior falls to the floor, blood pooling around his forehead.

Lily gasps a broken cry as Nico stands stunned in the spot, staring emptily down at his father.

He calmly walks over to Lily and sits opposite her. He looks disheveled and shell-shocked, broken.

LILY

I sit speechless at the events that have just unfolded before me. Nico sits opposite me, looking the same way he'd looked when I'd lost the baby. He looks empty and broken.

"Nico, are you okay?" My body shakes.

He stares at me blankly, then shakes his head slowly.

He sits a little straighter and looks toward Reece. "Jacob, I'm going to need your help. Can you do that for me?"

"Yeah, of course, Nicky. What do you need?" Reece asks quietly.

"I need you to send me the cargo location as soon as you leave here, no excuses. You hear me?"

"Sure, I swear it!"

I look to Nico, confused, as he starts to untie my legs and hands. "Abi, I need you to do something for me too."

My eyes meet his and he looks at me softly, his eyes filled with care and compassion as he gently strokes my hands. When he realizes what he's doing, he lets go of my hands and blows out a breath, overcome with emotion.

I'm in utter shock at what's occurring. I've gone from being panicked for my and my son's life to being set free.

Nico lifts my hand and wraps it around his gun, covering my hand with his own.

"You need to shoot me. I'm going to tell my guards that the guard on the floor shot me and my father. You're going to take my car keys..." He pushes a set of keys into my hand. "You will only have approximately ten to fifteen minutes head start. I will do my best to delay them. Drive toward the city, dump my car, it has a tracker. Get in a taxi and live your life, you understand me?" he says in an authoritative tone.

I can't speak, tears fill my eyes. I'm not sure why, so many reasons why.

"Okay," I agree weakly. Nico sits straighter and without any further warning, he presses the trigger of the gun, hitting directly into his stomach. "Fuck!" he spits through clenched teeth. I drop back into the chair, stunned. It's the first time I've ever shot a gun at someone. My whole body shakes, vibrations running through me.

"Go!" He waves his hand to Reece, who helps me up from the chair, dragging me up with my arm over his shoulder. We make our way toward the back door. The knife still in my leg, causing agony with every step.

"Abi..."

I spin around at Nico's words. "I'm sorry!" he says remorsefully.

I nod. "I know." I gently offer him a small smile. He returns it and then nods his head toward the door.

EPILOGUE

A round 18 Months Later

Cal

I'm sitting around the poker table on a Friday night in Bren's apartment with my brothers. After a stressful week, I'm finally starting to unwind, the beer is flowing, and the peanuts and chips on the table are being demolished at a rapid rate.

Finn is passing his toothpick from one side of his mouth to the other at a quickening pace, a tell-tale sign his poker hand is shit. Oscar has the best poker face of all of us, no fucker can ever get a read on him.

Con sits with a smug fucking grin. He can't hide his cocky jovial excitement that is bound to be a good hand. Bren throws down his cards dramatically. "I'm out! Shit hand again!"

I stifle a laugh as I lay my cards out proudly. I have a full house, but Con has wiped the floor with us again, somehow managing to get a royal flush. Both Finn and Oscar throw their cards into the center of the table.

"So I notice you managed to get out without Reece tagging along." Bren chuckles.

"Damn fucking right, I did. I love my kid to bits but, counting fucking cards? Crafty little fucker. Did you know he did that, Oscar?"

Oscar's smirk curls into the corner of his mouth. " 'Course not."

I narrow my eyes at him. Why do I not fucking believe him? "You, sneaky little fucker, you knew, didn't you?" I query while watching his face for a reaction, anything.

Oscar shrugs. "Might have taught him a trick or two."

The table erupts with accusations and "what the fucks."

"You've been counting cards this whole damn time?" Connor accuses.

"That's a load of bullshit. He never wins," Finn rightly states, shaking his head at Oscar.

Oscar just sits lazily back in his chair, smug, with his arms crossed over his chest. "I was making sure not to be too obvious," he deadpans back.

We all look at each other, absolutely fucking flabbergasted. All this fucking time and we didn't know.

"Where is the little shit tonight, anyway?" Con asks, changing the subject.

"Well after the shitstorm at school last week, his teachers declared they were putting Reece and Boris together for some project or other, to help them work out their differences and work better together." I air quote the latter part.

"Boris? The Russian kid?" Finn asks with his eyebrows furrowing together.

"Yeah, they've actually got on well this week and Lily's

relieved as fuck. I swear to god the tension at home has been off the fucking charts, what with all this hormone bullshit she's spouting. Anyway, Reece is at Boris's house tonight, working on a History project with him."

"Ah, it all makes sense now!" Oscar surmises.

"What does?"

"Reece came to me for additional surveillance cameras. One can now assume they've been planted at Boris's house." Oscar shrugs nonchalantly.

"Fuck!" I scrub my hand down my face. Lily would blow a fucking gasket if she thought Reece was doing anything other than a fucking History project. Instead, the little shit is surveying his opponent and no doubt the newfound friendship is bullshit too.

"What's with the hormone bullshit then?" Finn asks, breaking me away from my thoughts.

"Lily thinks her supersonic hormones are the reason why she got knocked up while on the pill, so now she thinks she must be super fucking fertile or something for it to happen twice. So she's making me fucking suit up every goddamn time we have sex." The disgust is oozing out of me.

"Can you believe that shit? She's not satisfied with normal fucking condoms, no, I have to have the thickest, heaviest fuckers there are. I swear to god, my balls are still blue after. It's like fucking torture knowing what she feels like without them and now having to go back to them. I feel like some fucking teenager, fumbling to get the damn thing on before I shoot my load, looking at her all…" I shake my head, not wanting to tell my brothers how insanely hot my wife's pussy looks.

My brothers start laughing around me. The little shits are enjoying my sexual demise. Who'd have thought when I originally hatched my plan to knock up my Mrs. that it would end up with me having to go back to fucking basics?

"Well at least her tits are bigger since having Chloe. That's a little bonus to soften the blow." Finn laughs at his own fucking joke.

I grit my teeth. "Very fucking funny. They might look bigger, but I can assure you I can't get anywhere near those beauties," I tell them all with a pointed look.

Gasps leave my brothers' mouths as their eyebrows shoot up. Con has a look of repulsion. "Why the fuck not?"

My hands jiggle in front of my chest for emphasis. "Because they hurt her like fucking crazy, her tits look like they're gonna explode, her nipples are fucking cracked and raw, like fucking blood dripping from them. Seriously never thought I'd say it myself, but they look pretty fucking nasty!" I blanch at the thought of Lily's pain.

Con grimaces. "Jesus, remind me to never knock a chick up!"

Finn laughs. "Like that's ever going to fucking happen. Don't you use those thick fucking condoms Cal is talking about? Did Lily raid your stash?" He chuckles to himself.

Con throws a peanut at Finn's head. "No, dipshit, she didn't. I need extra large ones and Cal here needs the small." He tugs on his crotch as he laughs at his own joke.

"So, no tits, and no bareback. Remind me why the fuck you love this family thing so much?"

"Shut the fuck up Finn, you wouldn't understand." I shake my head.

"I take it you're not planning on letting Lily know you swapped her pill out for fertility-enhancing drugs then?" Oscar deadpans.

"You know I'm fucking not. Now shut the fuck up with

the judgmental bullshit before you get me fucking banned from sex altogether."

Oscar's lips quirk up again. He was not a fan of my original plan. He has far too much respect for Lily and he doesn't like me not being completely honest with her.

Bren breaks the tension and the silence that has built around the table. "So, the little charity event I attended Tuesday was interesting." His eyebrows do a little wiggle.

"You got laid?" Con is first to ask.

"I got a hot piece of ass's cell number that I might call, but I was referring to seeing Connors ex-girlfriend looking all hot on stage and giving a speech." He whistles through his teeth to emphasize the hotness of the woman.

Con doesn't bat an eye at Bren's blatant effort to rile him. "Funny, I don't recall having an ex-girlfriend. Conquests, yes. Girlfriends, no!" He casually picks up a handful of peanuts and pops one in his mouth, giving Bren a wink.

Bren isn't finished with winding Connor up. "That's funny. Could have sworn you once had a feisty little brunette hanging off your shoulder constantly, a few years ago." He shrugs.

Finn and I look to one another, glancing at Oscar, who's also looking confused. Bren looks way too happy with his declaration and sits taller with a smug-as-fuck grin on his face. Connor sits up a little straighter. "What the fuck are you talking about?"

"You mean who the fuck am I talking about?" Bren counters cockily.

"Bren," I warn. "Cut the fucking shit."

Bren sighs. "Okay, so I'm sitting at a boring as fuck charity event for Survivors of Domestic Abuse when who should walk on stage and give a speech? One of their representatives, which just so happens to be Will, and fuck does she look hot!"

Silence, absolute and utter silence. Never has a poker night had silence like this before. Not even after Reece had declared he'd seen Oscar sterilizing a vibrator.

"Fuuck," Finn groans, breaking the silence.

Con is white, so fucking pale he looks sick. "Will, as in Will."

"Yeah man, it was her. Honest to god. She had us all eating out the palm of her fucking hand, she looked stunning too." Bren laughs to himself, oblivious of the tension in the room. "Seriously, you'd have blown your fucking load at the table, Con."

"Will?"

I palm my hand down my face. Fuck, this was going to be hard work.

Bren chuckles. "Yeah, Will! Jesus, Con, if I thought you were going to go all fucking mushy in the head, I wouldn't have bothered telling you."

"She was at a Survivors of Domestic Abuse event as a key spokesperson?" Oscar says, ever the sensible voice of reason.

Con jumps up from his chair, making it crash to the floor. Here we go...

He points his finger sharply at Bren. "You went there Tuesday night and it's now Friday. Why the hell did you wait until now to tell me this? And what fucking domestic violence? What the fuck did she have to say? Who was she with?" Con paces frantically, glaring daggers at Bren, pushing his hands through his hair in temper.

"Calm down, Con. Come on, it might not be what you're thinking." I try to placate him.

"Look man, I really don't know much and if I'm being

brutally honest, I didn't hear anything she had to fucking say. I was a little taken aback by her being there, on the stage, looking so hot and that. The crowd liked her, though." He exhales, completely oblivious to the hole he's digging.

"Waste. Of. Fucking. Space," Oscar snaps.

"Well, how the fuck was I meant to know he'd go all fucking goo-ga over her? Last I knew, they had a fucking break up, which was probably his fucking fault being a dick to her as per usual. The poor girl must have come to her senses and got the fuck out of town."

Oh shit, he did not just say that.

Connor fucking *roars* across the table, peanuts and chips flying, beer bottles hitting the table and floor. Finn grabs hold of his shoulders to restrain him. Bren sits frozen at the table in the same spot, either asking for more trouble or utterly gobsmacked at Connor, who is normally so laid back he's horizontal.

Oscar jumps up from his chair, snapping and getting our attention. "Enough! I can access the fucking events guest list, find the guest speakers and representatives, and you can have her information by the morning, okay? No fucking harm done."

Con slowly relaxes against Finn, his face red with rage and his teeth caught in his bottom lip. He holds his hands up for Finn to release him. I don't think any of us have seen him show such weakness, especially toward a female.

Bren looks up from the table. "Look man, I'm sorry, okay? I didn't realize you still harbored feelings there. If I'd have known..."

Connor straightens his shirt, turns his back, and marches out the door, slamming it for emphasis.

We all look to one another, eyebrows raised. "I mean, I

know he beats himself up over her but not anything like that," Finn declares, breathing out with frustration.

I take a deep breath. "Yeah, I know things run deeper than he ever lets on. Things are about to get fucking messy, that's for sure!"

THE END

AFTERWORD

Did you enjoy reading CAL?
Please consider leaving a review!
It can be as long or short as you like and will help place my
book in the hands of a new reader.

CONTACT

For all news on upcoming books, visit my Facebook page:
Reckless Readers Facebook Group

Instagram: BJ Alpha

ACKNOWLEDGMENTS

I must start with where it all began, TL Swan. When I started reading your books, I never realized I was in a place I needed pulling out of. Your stories brought me back to myself.

With your constant support and the network created as 'Cygnet Inkers' I was able to create something I never realized was possible, I genuinely thought I'd had my day. You made me realize tomorrow is just the beginning.

For that I am eternally grateful!

To the Cygnet Inkers, thank you! For always being there, for answering the dumbest of questions and for never judging. I honestly could not have achieved this without you!

JC Hawke, thank you for supporting my meltdown with my Front Cover.

Rhiannon Marina, where do I start? You've achieved so much yourself but you're always just a message away to offer me support and guidance. Thank you, without you I'd have given up so many times.

Thank you to my Beta Readers love you so much!

My sensitivity readers Jaclyn, Tanya and J, thank you immensely for your support and reassurance.

To my breakfast club ladies, you may not realize it's me yet but when you do, thank you for all your love and support in day-to-day life.

Thank you, Kami, for being there with the multitude of silly questions I ask you about America in general.

Thank you to https://autism.org.uk for the wealth of information available to me and many others.

To my boys, thank you for everything.

To my hubby, the J in my BJ. Thank you for pushing me, listening to me and supporting me through this whole process. Without you I wouldn't be BJ Alpha. Love you trillions!

ALSO BY B J ALPHA

90615332R00144